Copyright © 2022 E S Monk

Published 2022

ISBN 9798392986156

Seal Cove

By

E.S. Monk

For

Beryl

Kate

Kate's shrill alarm bleeped incessantly through the pitch-black early morning hour until her fumbling hand finally managed to flick her bedside lamp on and switch it off. She slipped out of bed and swiftly dressed. She was on a tight schedule today. Padding down the stairs, she was hit with the welcoming aroma of fresh coffee and hot buttered toast. She smiled to herself; her dad always got up the extra hour early on market day to make sure she had a proper breakfast before the long day ahead.

"Morning Dad," she whispered, keen not to wake her sleeping sister, as she took her seat at their farmhouse kitchen table.

"Morning love," he replied, dropping a kiss on top of her head before placing her breakfast in front of her. "I thought you'd be up early. I checked the weather last night! Clear and dry with only a light breeze."

She smiled in reply at his thoughtfulness. Between mouthfuls of toast, she said, "You're right, as always! I'm going to take Artie out for a quick blast across the beach before I head off."

"After I drop Jodie to school, I'll be up in the top field for most of the day," her dad announced. "I don't have to pick her up, she's staying with one of her friends tonight. A stretch of fencing needs some repairs and it's looking like two cows are close to calving, so I can keep an eye on them whilst I'm there."

Kate then watched him pack up the three lunch boxes he had been preparing before she joined him in the kitchen. "Put it in the Land Rover on your way out," he insisted, "I don't want you to forget it!"

"I will, Dad. Thank you." She swigged her last drop of coffee, then pulled on her battered old leather riding boots and headed out into the grey half-light of dawn.

She heard Artie nicker as she approached his paddock. She had to fit her riding in around her heavy work schedule, so he was well used to being ridden at any given hour of the day. She called to him softly and he was ready and waiting by the time she arrived at the gateway. She never bothered with a head collar for him; he knew the drill and always seemed happy to oblige with their haphazard routine. She stroked his nose and felt his warm breath on her fingers.

"Come on then boy," she whispered, then unlatched the gate. They walked quietly, side-by-side towards the stable block, the other horses sleepily acknowledging the early morning goings on of the yard.

Artie stopped politely outside the tack room and waited patiently for Kate to bring out a slice of hay for him to munch whilst she tended to the breakfast and morning routine for all the other horses. She smiled at her horse. Horses came and went at her yard, but Artie was hers, and he knew it. Arthur, known as Artie to his nearest and dearest, was a jet black, 15.3, ten-year-old gelding. He was at the peak of fitness, with rippling muscles, and he positively oozed power and grace. And he knew that he was lord of the yard. He was quiet and kind, sensible and well-mannered, but he had an air about him that told every other horse on the yard that Kate was his, and that they shouldn't go getting any ideas above their station, and they never did when he was around.

Arthur's best friends were Pumpkin, Jodie's horse, and Cupcake, who had been the girls' first pony. They were both permanent residents on the yard. The sisters always worried about mixing clients' horses and market horses with their own herd. There was always the fear of friendships being formed then broken or diseases being spread, and so Artie, Pumkin and Cupcake were kept separate, forming their own little herd, and most often kept themselves to themselves.

Kate checked her watch. She had exactly one hour before she needed to leave. Hastily grooming then tacking up her horse, she mounted, and set off down the farm track. She liked riding in the morning. The air was clear and fresh, and Artie always had a bounce in his step. They crossed three fields of their own farmland, and she noted the small herd of her father's cattle grazing quietly. She felt a warm fuzzy feeling inside at the thought of new life on the farm any day now.

Kate and Artie then followed the track along the cliff tops. The spectacular view of the awe-inspiring ocean never failed to bring a smile to her face. Artie slowly and carefully plodded down the narrow coastal path, and as was their routine, stopped at just the right place for her to look down into the private, inaccessible cove where the local wild seals lived. She watched them for a moment, bobbing about in the water. They were such elegant creatures in the water but so ungainly on land! She smiled as she watched one slip out of the water and wobble its way onto the sand.

A gentle squeeze of her legs told Artie that her seal spotting was over, and it was time to continue. They clip-clopped along in silence until the overgrown path levelled out and sand met with grassland. The tide was out, and the far-reaching sands were empty, as she knew they would be at this early hour. She guided Artie along the seaside track parallel to the beach for three quarters of a mile. Between his two little black ears she could see the burnt orange glow of the sun beginning to rise and the white foamy waves lapping on the sand. She directed him off the path and down onto the beach until his hooves were splashing in the chilly water. Turning for home she had a clear view of the jagged, rough Cornish cliff tops, and although they held an element of rugged wildness about them, Kate always thought they carried a sort of beauty in them as well. Artie's ears pricked, and she felt his excitement build for what was to come.

"Are you ready, boy?" she said out loud to her horse. And with a squeeze of her legs, he moved into his powerful forward trot. "Let's go!" she called out, and as her horse transitioned into canter, and then swiftly into a fast gallop, she could feel the wind whipping around her unruly red hair and taste the salty tang of the ocean as she and Arthur flew across the barren beach.

The walk home cooled Artie down and after a quick kiss on his nose, she turned him back out into his paddock with Pumpkin and Cupcake. She noticed that whilst she'd been gone her dad had hitched the horsebox to the Land Rover for her and parked it facing the farm entrance, all ready to go. She marched up to the kitchen window and saw that Jodie was now up and munching her breakfast, and between mouthfuls, she was chatting animatedly to her father. Kate tapped loudly on it to get their attention, then smiled and waved and gave her dad a thumbs up in thanks for hitching up her box. Climbing into the Land Rover, she saw her lunch on the passenger seat, before remembering that she had left it on the kitchen table whilst putting her boots on. Good old Dad!

Kate loved market day. The hustle and bustle of people, some familiar, and some not, and the excitement of choosing new horses to train and then sell on. It was as much a social event as it was about business for the farmers and equestrians who spent many days alone on their isolated farms. Although she and her father ran their two-hundred-acre farm together, he dealt with the cattle and arable side of things, and she the horses. She took in clients' horses for backing and training, but what she loved most was starting a horse from scratch, before anyone else had made a mess of them. It was always much easier for her to start with a blank canvas rather than fix someone else's mistakes and the terrible results of poor horsemanship.

She weaved her way through the crowd towards the makeshift stalls that the horses for sale were secured in before the auction began. Her notebook and pencil in hand, she slowly walked up and down each aisle of horses, noting the numbers of the potentials, and marking a big X next to the ones that were a definite no. After narrowing her options down, she felt confident that she would secure the purchase of the two horses that she needed today. She'd found four possible candidates. Now all that was left to do was take her place alongside the sales ring and wait for the auction to begin, crossing her fingers that she would not be outbid on her selected horses.

Kate sat up straight when the little filly she liked the look of entered the ring.

"15.1, unbacked, three-and-a-half-year-old, bright bay filly," announced the auctioneer.

The filly skipped and danced around the ring, frightened of the unfamiliar environment that she had unwillingly been thrust into. The auctioneer encouraged the sale, but the unbacked, spirited filly was not doing herself any favours with her skittish behaviour. Kate grinned to herself and nodded at the auctioneer. And after a flutter of interest, which soon dwindled away, the auctioneer called out "sold" to Kate. She was pleased with her purchase, especially as the filly fetched a lower price than Kate had originally budgeted for her.

Next came the 16.2 unbacked four-year-old grey gelding that Kate had taken a liking to. He had good bone, a leg in each corner type, he appeared calm and steady in his stall and had a very unusual, inky black, half-moon shaped marking on his left shoulder. However, it was not meant to be. Kate was a businesswoman, and unless it was to do with her beloved Artie, she ruled with her head, not her heart. She bid keenly, but he was a lovely horse and there was an opposing bidder. Yet, although she'd swivelled in her seat, looking in every direction, she could not spot them, despite her keen eye for spotting the understated actions of other proficient bidders. But to her disappointment her eagle eyes could not detect any subtle gestures from anyone. Kate, slightly disheartened, bowed out gracefully as soon as her budget was exceeded.

Kate's disappointment did not last long, though. A lovely unbacked four-year-old cob entered the ring who she'd not seen on her earlier inspection. He must have been a late arrival, she tutted to herself. He was a stamp of a chap at 15.3 hands, skewbald in colour and she sensed a willingness about him as he was being led around the ring and a softness in his liquid brown eyes. Although her client had requested a horse just over the 16-hand mark, she felt that him being just one inch shy of that should not be too much of a problem, especially as he had a regal stance about him, giving off the impression that he was bigger than he actually was. And with the filly being under budget, she managed to secure his purchase with the left-over money. All in all, Kate felt like she'd had a successful day.

After sorting out the necessary legal paperwork and payment in the stuffy, cramped sales office, and then loading the horses, it was four o'clock by the time she climbed into her Land Rover. Her eyes fell greedily on her lunch box. She had been focused, purposeful and business-like at the sale, her mind only on the task at hand. But now, with the adrenaline and excitement slowly fading away, she was feeling ravenous, and gratefully tucked into her homemade ham salad sandwich.

She licked the sugar off her fingers from the slice of homemade Victoria sponge cake.

Jodie really can bake! she thought fondly of her seventeen-year-old sister.

Then she started her car and slowly eased her way out of the busy carpark. She couldn't wait to get home and tell her dad about her day and the new residents for the yard.

Jonah

Jonah waited as the passport officer at Plymouth dockyard looked him up and down before glancing back at his passport photo. A grim nod from the officer confirmed his identity before thrusting his passport back into his hand.

"Next," the man barked.

Jonah had been dismissed and was free to go. He weaved his way between the throng of passengers, headed straight through the sliding glass doors and finally set foot on English soil for the first time in seven years.

Dawn was rising as streaks of yellow trickled through the murky grey clouds of the Devonshire coastline. Car horns beeped, engines revved, and staff and passengers shouted to each other over the dockyard city noise. Jonah couldn't stand it. It was a far cry from the picturesque French port of Brittany where he'd boarded the ferry the night before. The pretty town of Roscoff boasted charm and classic French elegance. He'd enjoyed strolling past the picture-perfect coastal cottages and full bloomed gardens and soaking up the peaceful atmosphere whilst inhaling the delicate floral scent on his way to the efficiently run little French port.

He slipped his passport into the secure inner pocket of his backpack, the backpack that contained the entirety of his worldly goods, then heaved it on to his shoulders, and with his head down, marched purposefully over to the bus station. After a somewhat hectic thirty minutes of the dockyard bus driving through the busy city of Plymouth, and Jonah changing buses at the city central depot, he finally sat back in his seat and rested. His mind settled, knowing that he had made it. All he could do now was wait. He would be there in just under two hours.

He looked out of the window and watched the city smog fade away as the bus bumbled over the Tamar bridge and into Cornwall. Rolling countryside replaced the concrete blocks, and the lush green fields, dotted with livestock, brought a smile to his face. It was a strong gut instinct that had encouraged him to return to England, and it continued to burn inside him now. He had no fathomable explanation for it, just a strong desire to return that he couldn't ignore, and ever since he saw the advert announcing the date and time of the Cornish livestock market, his drive to return had intensified.

Jonah had been one of life's drifters for as long as he could remember. Ever since his mother, God rest her soul, had dragged herself to the hospital, with Jonah in tow, and after handing him over to one of the nurses, had collapsed. She suffered with a heart defect and had been warned that bearing children would cause too much strain on her already delicate heart. When she accidentally fell pregnant with Jonah, she had been adamant about keeping her baby. The doctors had supported her wishes and done everything they could to ensure a safe birth for both her and her son. But the birth had been traumatic, and just like the doctors had warned her, she never fully recovered. Eighteen months later her weakened, damaged heart could go on no more and she passed away at the feet of the hospital nurse. Little Jonah had then spent his entire youth in the care system, bouncing between one foster home and another. Some were nice, and some not so nice. It was all much of a muchness to Jonah. He stayed a few months in one home, then he moved on to the next, and half the time he never even bothered to unpack his battered little rucksack.

On turning eighteen, he was finally released from the system. Along with some of the other foster lads he'd got to know along the way, he rented a small place in the centre of Manchester. Then, they waited for their lives to begin. Except they didn't. With no family, support, or guidance, they didn't know how to succeed in the outside world. They all worked part- time jobs, bar jobs, labouring and the like, to fund their drinking and partying. Petty crime wasn't off the cards either. Anything to make an extra quid or two was all fair game to Jonah and his mates, but as the years slowly ticked by, Jonah began to think that being on first name terms with the local coppers might not be as funny as he and his mates first thought.

At twenty-two, he was bunking in with a couple of rough and readies. He knew they were even more dodgy than himself, but he needed a place to crash and theirs was the only forthcoming offer. It was then that his gut instinct began to ring out loud and clear, so much so that he knew he couldn't block it out anymore. He knew they were dealing drugs, and in the beginning, he had managed to stay out of it, but they were getting pushier and pushier as the days went by. For all of Jonah's faults, of which there were many in his youth, drugs had never been his thing, and hanging around outside school gates pushing them on to unsuspecting youngsters was something he would never be a part of.

Coming home late one night from his shift at the pub, he saw his grotty little flat swarming with police. He knew there and then that if he ever went back there, he would be caught up in the whole drug dealing mess and find himself in prison for something he didn't even do. For the first time in his life, he allowed his instincts to guide him. With only his wallet and phone in his pocket, and his mother's locket tied on a piece of leather around his neck, he walked away. He headed to the coach station and bought a ticket for the first coach out of there.

He stayed on that coach, for hour after hour, until the driver announced they were arriving in Salisbury, their final stop. The first thing Jonah had done was head into the city centre to find a camping shop. He bought a rucksack, sleeping bag and a waterproof coat were purchased, then he headed to the supermarket to buy a spare pair of jeans, a shirt and some boxershorts, along with some food. He packed up his bag, heaved it on to his shoulders, and walked.

It was early summer as he headed away from the busy town and aimlessly trudged along the idyllic Dorset country lanes. At night, he would find a secluded, quiet corner of a field, or a patch of woodland off the beaten track, and there he would bed down, grateful that the summer evenings were dry and warm. For nine days he aimlessly walked, with nowhere to be and nowhere to go, and he revelled in the solitude and found a real appreciation for all the natural beauty that the countryside held. After nine days, the weather broke, unleashing heavy rain and gale force winds, and he sought shelter in what he presumed was an abandoned, derelict barn.

Snuggled up in his sleeping bag, enjoying the sound of the wind howling and the rain hammering on the rickety barn walls, Jonah was startled when the big burly farmer, and owner of the barn, came tumbling through the door. He was leaking wet and breathing heavily with the exertion of carrying a very large sheep. He didn't notice Jonah straight away, and Jonah watched quietly as he settled the ewe and muttered soothingly to her. And it was on that night that the course of Jonah's life changed forever.

After the farmer got over the initial shock of finding Jonah in his barn on that stormy night, and learnt his current situation, Mr and Mrs Peterson had welcomed him into their farm with open arms in return for his help over the harvest season. The pay was meagre, but Jonah didn't mind. He had a warm bed, and a permanently full stomach, thanks to Mrs Peterson's wonderful cooking. And what's more, he learned. He learned everything he could about farming life and working with the livestock and land. And he found his true calling when he met Peppermint, Mrs Peterson's mare. Being a born and bred city boy he'd never had any interaction with horses before, but the first time he placed his hand on Peppermint's velvety soft muzzle, he felt it. A connection with another sentient being that he'd never felt before. Once the harvest was over, and on Mr and Mrs Peterson's recommendation that he should get out into the world and live life to the full, he applied for a passport, and with the wages he earned over the summer, he bought a one-way ticket to America.

At the age of twenty-three, his life was finally beginning. He knew when he left the comfort of Mr and Mrs Peterson's farm that he would never see them again, but he left them a note on his parting, explaining what they had both done for him and how he would never forget their kindness.

Three years he spent in America, working and travelling from ranch to ranch, learning all he could about horses and farming. He spent the next two years in New Zealand, then eighteen months in Australia.

After that, his wandering soul had brought him to Europe, and that was where he had been for the last six months. He knew, deep down, that he was steadily making his way back to England, because something inside him was telling him that it was time for him to go home. Ever since he first placed his hand on Peppermint, he knew that he wanted his own horse. As much as Peppermint seemed to enjoy his company and their many rides out over the Dorset countryside, she was Mrs Peterson's horse, not his. And it was the same with all the other horses he'd worked and trained over the years; their loyalty and trust were never fully his. And now, he felt that it was time for him to take that risk and build a permanent relationship with something other than his backpack.

The livestock sale in Cornwall, announcing both cattle and horses for sale, had glared at him like a bright red beacon when it flashed up on his phone during a Google search. For such a seasoned traveller, he knew very little of his own country other than Manchester and the tiny idyllic pocket of Dorset where Mr and Mrs Peterson's farm was situated. Cornwall held the appeal of rugged clifftops, beautiful beaches, and far stretching moorland, including the novelty of wild Cornish ponies.

And as usual, with nowhere to go and nowhere to be, Jonah followed his instincts and booked his ferry ticket to Plymouth with the intention of arriving at the Cornish livestock market. And then he would just wait and see to where he might end up.

The bus pulled into a little Cornish town as the driver announced that it was his last stop, and everyone must now disembark his bus. The market was held just outside of the town, and after listening carefully to the driver's detailed directions, Jonah pulled his backpack onto his shoulders and set off.

The market was a hive of activity when he arrived. Some of the farmers were huddled in groups, sipping hot cups of takeaway tea, and chatting amongst themselves before the auction began. Others were strolling up and down the aisles of penned livestock, taking notes and scrutinising the stock with experienced eyes.

Jonah headed straight to the horses. The first horse to draw him in for a closer look was a bright bay filly. He could see that she had spirit and fire in her belly, but on closer inspection, he noticed her to be only three and a half years old, too young to be backed immediately by someone of his muscular build and six-foot frame. And so, with reluctance, he moved on. And then he saw him. A handsome, well-built grey gelding, with an unusual inky black half-moon marking on his left shoulder. As soon as his fingers touched his silky soft nose, and he felt the warmth of his breath on his hand, he knew. His deep-rooted gut instincts had brought him to this very place, for this specific moment in time, to meet this horse.

Jonah positioned himself at the top of the staggered auction ring. It gave him a good view of the crowd, and a clear view for the auctioneer to see his bids when the time came, but it also kept him away from the main hub. He leant against the wall and watched. His attention was piqued when the little filly entered the ring, and he watched her dance and prance on the end of the handler's rope. And he watched the determined red-headed young woman smile with triumph when she won the bidding. And then he felt his pulse quicken when his horse entered the ring. Once the bidding got into full swing, he felt a flicker of annoyance that the red-headed woman was bidding against him. She had already purchased the filly that he couldn't have, and although he could see that she was tall, she was slim with it, and nowhere near his height, so the filly would be perfectly capable of carrying her when the time came. He was also reluctantly impressed at the woman's choice in horses; she seemed to know which were the cream of the crop out of the selection on offer. He continued to bid with a steely determination, until finally she relented, and the grey horse became his.

His name was Jonty. It was plain and simple, and Jonah liked it. And so, holding the rope attached to his new horse's head collar, his rucksack on his back, they set off with a spring in their step. The Cornish countryside was calling them and there were adventures to be had.

Kate

Kate turned down the driveway, eager to unload and settle the new horses in, excitement bubbling up inside her for their training to begin. She was surprised to see Flo, her father's dog, sitting stock still in her parking spot. The dog carefully moved out of the way as she brought the Land Rover to a stop, and then she began bouncing up and down at her driver's side door.

"Hello, you," said Kate, bending down to give her a stroke. "Where's dad?" she asked the dog, looking around her. Like most farm dogs, she was never usually far from her master's side.

Flo span in circles, bounding forwards and backwards and getting herself under Kate's feet.

"You silly girl," Kate giggled. Then she strode over to the horse box, opened the latch, and dropped the tail board down. Flo continued to bounce in front of her, almost as if she was trying to entice her to follow her, and still, Kate could not see her father anywhere.

"Ok, girl," Kate said softly to the dog. "Let me put the horses away and then I'll come with you."

Flo watched her intently, as if she understood, and as soon as both horses were secured in their new stables, the spinning and bounding started again. Kate involuntary shivered. Flo was displaying such unusual behaviour, and it gave Kate a strong sense of foreboding. As soon as Kate's focus was on Flo, the dog took off down the track before slipping through a gateway into a field. Kate had to run to keep up with her, and she was breathless as she clambered over the second gate.

"Slow down Flo," she called out, as the dog effortlessly launched herself over the stone wall before disappearing from view. Kate scrambled after her, and once standing on top of the wall she had a clear view of the top field where the pregnant cows were grazing. And then she saw him. Her father was lying flat out in the middle of the field.

"Dad," she screamed at the top of her lungs. Panic swarmed through her as she ran as fast as she could to her father.

Flo lay down next to him, and with her body pressed up against him, she looked imploringly at Kate.

"Good girl, Flo," Kate said. Then she whispered, "Dad, it's me, Kate. Can you hear me?"

Her father grumbled and stirred at the sound of her voice. "Kate, I knew I could hold on long enough to see you."

"Oh Dad, what's happened? Let me help you up." Kate slipped her arms underneath him.

"No," said her father. "I can't get up."

Kate's heart pounded in her chest as her father gasped for breath.

"It's my time, Kate," he continued, in an unfamiliar raspy voice. "Flo lay down beside me and kept me warm with her own body heat." He reached out and gave his dog an affectionate stroke. "Always loyal, my Flo. My time has come, Kate, and there's nowhere else I would rather be than out here, on my own land, at peace. Your mother is waiting for me, and I must go to her now."

Tears sprung into Kate's eyes. Her throat burned, and her heart ached on realising that her father was dying right before her eyes.

"Dad, please," she begged, wrapping her arms around him. "I can get help, I can get a doctor. Please, Dad, don't leave me."

"It's ok," he replied, his breathing beginning to steady. "It's ok, my girl. My beautiful, spirited girl. The farm is now yours, and your sister's. Tell Jodie I love her. And you, my darling Kate, I love you."

As Kate held her father in her arms, she felt him take his last breath, and then he was gone. Here, in the middle of his favourite field, the field where new life was delivered year in, year out from his beloved cows, this was now the place where her father was taken from her. His body lay limp in her arms as she cradled him and slowly began to realise that with her father now gone, both the farm business and her own horse training business were her responsibility. The thought of her little sister losing both of her parents at such a young age, and how she would now be the sole provider and guardian of her, weighed heavily on her shoulders.

She didn't know how long she held her father, but the sun was all but set when she eased her cold, aching limbs off the ground and slowly walked, with Flo at her side, all the way back to her empty farmhouse and called the emergency services.

The ambulance arrived within the hour, and in a daze, Kate explained all she could to the two kind, sympathetic paramedics. They explained that they would have to take the body away, so that a doctor could certify the death. They informed her that someone would be in contact with her soon to make the necessary arrangements for his funeral.

Kate's father had always been adamant that Flo lived downstairs, and not once had she ever set foot even on the first step of their staircase. But that evening, as grief swelled through her being, she called Flo to follow her upstairs. Throughout the darkest hours of that night, Kate held on to her father's best friend and wept for hour upon hour, clinging on to the dog's living, breathing body, and Kate knew that Flo needed her, just as much as she needed Flo.

Neither Kate nor Flo slept that night, and when her alarm finally rang out loud and clear in the still air, they both heaved themselves out of bed. There was work to be done, and they were both grateful for the distraction and their daily routine to begin. Kate completed her morning horse chores on autopilot, and with Flo constantly at her side, she filled up her dad's battered old Land Rover with bags of feed, then set off across the fields to feed the stock and check on the heavily pregnant cows. She stopped the car and watched quietly as a newborn, healthy calf suckled its mother. New life had appeared, exactly in the same place that her father had passed away the night before. The circle of life continues, she mused, before the tears spilled again with the thought that she would never share such a sight with her father again.

Kate had made the decision last night to go to Jodie's school and explain to them what had happened, and then take Jodie home. She did not want gossip spreading and she certainly did not want Jodie to hear the tragic news of their father from anyone else but her, and maybe for slightly selfish reasons, she wanted to get it over and done with. And so, she told herself that the safest way to ensure this was to get to her first, and once all her morning chores were complete, she and Flo set off.

Jodie's head teacher was kind, sympathetic and completely understanding. Kate couldn't stand it. She knew she was being irrational and unfair, but the looks of pity drove her crazy, and as soon as the teacher said she could collect Jodie, she hot footed it out of her office as fast as she could. Kate knew the layout of the school - she herself had attended the same school, albeit eleven years ago, so she found Jodie's classroom quickly. Kate tentatively knocked on the door, and the teacher beckoned her in, and she saw a look of surprise spring on to her sister's face at seeing her there.

After a brief, hushed explanation to Jodie's class teacher that there had been a family emergency, she was briskly strolling along the corridor, with Jodie skipping along beside her. Finally, she pushed open the school doors and breathed in the fresh air deeply.

"What is it, Kate? What's going on?" enquired Jodie.

"We're going riding," Kate announced, knowing that Jodie would need Pumpkin to support her once she found out what had happened.

"You've taken me out of school to go riding?" replied her baffled sister.

"Yes," she stated in her big sisterly matter of fact tone, and somehow Jodie knew not to push. They travelled in silence until they reached home. Jodie announced that she would change into her riding clothes, then meet Kate on the yard.

Kate tacked up Artie and Pumpkin quickly and was sitting on top of her horse by the time Jodie returned. Jodie mounted Pumpkin quietly, and with Flo trotting along at their heels, they set off down the farm track. They passed the gateway that Flo had taken Kate through the previous evening and continued along the track and around a corner. From their position on horseback, they could see over the hedge to where the cows were grazing over in the next field. Kate brought Artie to a halt, and that was when Jodie noticed Flo.

"Kate," she said with a tremble in her voice. "Why is Flo with us? Why was she with you when you picked me up? Where's Dad? Kate! Tell me now. What the hell is going on."

"He's gone," she said softly to her sister. And before Jodie had chance to interrupt her, she continued, "I found him over there when I got home yesterday." She pointed to the cow field. "He wasn't alone, Jodie. Flo stayed with him until she heard the Land Rover arrive back in the yard. It was her who showed me where to find him."

Kate looked at her sister, her face ghostly white as she tried to process the information she was giving her.

"He passed away in my arms. He was at peace, Jodie, and he told me to tell you that he loved you, but his time had come. He wanted to be with Mum. I'm so sorry, Jodie."

Jodie had still not uttered a word, so she gently asked Artie to walk on, and like she knew she would, Pumpkin fell into step behind him. The sisters remained silent as the horses plodded along the route they knew so well, all the way down to the beach, and just like she had done the previous morning, she directed Artie along the track parallel to the beach for three quarters of a mile. She looked over at

Jodie. Her beautiful little face was haunted with solemness.

"To the beach," she announced, as she guided Artie on to the sand. Kate and Jodie plodded along until they reached the shoreline, and then Kate turned Artie for home. Together, side by side, with Flo running alongside them, they asked their horses to canter. Kate could feel Artie building beneath her, and she could feel his power as she encouraged him to run as hard and as fast as he wanted to. She gave him a loose rein, and with his thundering hooves beneath her, and her sister galloping along at her side, she let her tears flow. The hurt and anger that had been simmering since the moment her father passed in her arms finally boiled over. She let out an animalistic shriek as she galloped along the barren beach, and then she heard her sister scream wildly beside her. They screamed and shouted until their voices hurt and their horses tired from their run.

Returning to a steady walk, they directed their horses towards home, and still, Jodie said nothing, and Kate knew that she must deal with her father's death in her own way.

Back on the yard, Kate untacked, groomed, and then turned Artie back out in his paddock, then told her sister she had to go and check on the cows. Her sister nodded but made no attempt at conversation. Kate walked away with Flo at her heels, leaving her sister to grieve with Pumpkin.

It was mid-afternoon when Jodie approached her.

"I'm going to meet Theo now. I won't be home too late," Jodie informed her, and then she turned without a backwards glance, and she headed back along the farm track to meet her friend.

Kate looked down at Flo, the faithful little collie dog that had not left her side since losing her master. She bent down and stroked her silky-smooth ears, then reached her arms around her and pulled her close. "Oh Flo, what are we going to do?" And with Flo unable to answer her, she simply buried her head in her fur and wept.

Jodie

Jodie stared glumly at herself in the bathroom mirror. She had officially been an orphan for six weeks. And twice now, she'd stood on the cliff top of Seal Cove, with Kate by her side and scattered the ashes of a parent, her tender heart aching as she watched them flitter so very far away from her in the Cornish sea breeze. She was seventeen and two months old and would now spend the rest of her life without the guidance and love of her parents. And if her lack of period for the last ten days and the three positive pregnancy tests she was clutching in her hand were anything to go by, she would be a parent herself in approximately seven months and two weeks. Nausea rose within her again, and crouching over the toilet bowl, she inelegantly threw up for the third time that morning.

After hastily dressing, she padded downstairs and tentatively peeked out of the kitchen window. She saw Kate in the makeshift schooling paddock working with her new auction horse, Philippa. Jodie's mouth felt dry, and sweat was prickling on her brow at the thought of telling her older sister that she was going to be an aunty. *There's no point putting it off*, she thought wryly. It wasn't like she could hide it. And truth be told, she was a little bit frightened about the prospect of having a baby. She'd lost her mother when she was only two years old in a boating accident. Her mother, along with her girlfriends, had taken a rare day off. Her father had wholeheartedly agreed that a day away from the farm and their two rambunctious daughters would do her the world of good. She'd kissed them all goodbye and smiled warmly, telling them all that she would be home soon and would make pancakes as a treat for dinner. Except she never did come home. The ever-unpredictable Cornish weather changed whilst the boat was far out at sea. A rescue party had been sent out, but they were too late. Two women were rescued, and two were not. Her mother had been drowned at sea. It had been her father and Kate who had raised her.

She knew that Kate would know what to do. Being eleven years older than her, she always did. She had patiently braided her hair just the way she liked it when she was little. It was Kate who had taught her how to ride and encouraged her father to let her have a horse of her own, and it was her who gave her the birds and the bees talk and was a shoulder to cry on when the boys at school were mean to her. And as if Kate didn't have enough problems to deal with, now Jodie was going to announce this unexpected surprise. She hoped, that once she'd calmed down, and lord knows how long that will take, she would know what to do.

Through the window she saw Kate lead Philippa out of the schooling area, the training session now finished, and with trepidation flowing through her veins she opened the front door and strolled over to the yard.

"You're up late! I've fed Pumpkin for you" said Kate, with a concerned look on her face. "In fact," she continued, studying her, "you don't look too well. You looked peaky yesterday, maybe I should take you to the doctors?"

Her sister's big green eyes were scrutinising her and she stammered, "Kate…Kate."

"What is it?" she asked kindly.

Here we go. "Kate, I'm pregnant."

"Wait. What? You're what?" Kate blurted out, bewilderment etched on her face.

"I'm going to have a baby, Kate," Jodie replied.

"But how? You don't even have a boyfriend. You told me you would come to me when you were ready. We talked about this, Jodie. I don't understand."

"I'm so sorry, Kate. I know it's a lot for you to take in, but I've taken the test. Three of them, in fact. I'm one hundred percent pregnant."

Her sister just stared at her; her mouth wide open but no words were coming out. Jodie shifted uncomfortably from foot to foot, waiting for the major telling off that she was sure to erupt out of her sister at any moment.

"I'm going riding," Kate announced, and Jodie watched her walk away to catch Artie from the field.

Jodie retraced her steps back to the farmhouse, flicked on the radio and busied herself in the kitchen. She loved to cook and bake and make house. She had asked her father last year if she could leave school after her GCSEs. She wanted to be at home to help on the farm and to take care of her dad and Kate, but he'd said no. He insisted that she go back to school and sit her A-levels. He'd insisted that she was too young to be tied to a kitchen sink!

Singing along quietly to the radio, she decided to make Kate some cupcakes. She would make Kate's favourite lemon ones with the buttercream icing, as a peace offering. She only hoped that they would not be thrown in her face when her sister returned. As she sifted flour and beat eggs, she let her mind wander back to the day that she knew without a doubt was the day she'd fallen pregnant.

It was the day Kate had told her their father had died. She'd been grateful that Kate told her when they were out riding. She'd needed the hard, fast gallop across the beach to release the sudden influx of emotions that imploded within her on hearing the devastating news. And being with Pumpkin afterwards had meant that her tears could flow freely, without her having to voice them to anyone. She didn't need to say anything to her mare. Pumpkin just knew that she needed to hold on to her tightly and let her anguish flow into her golden mane. After hours of being with only her horse, she then felt the need for human company. But not Kate's. She loved her sister, and she knew the time would come when they would talk over the practicalities of the business and farm, and that they would grieve their father together, but not right now. She needed someone outside of their family unit, and aside from Pumpkin, the only person she truly trusted was her best friend Theo.

She'd grown up with Theo. He was one year older than her and his family owned the neighbouring farm. As children they had run, played, and ridden their ponies with complete freedom over both farms, and when they became teenagers, it was with Theo that she first tried beer, and they had got drunk together on more than one occasion in his father's hay barn. And when one of the boys at school started bullying her, a stern word from the popular Theo in the year above soon put an end to it. Theo had left school last year. Theo's parents needed his help on their farm, and since he was an only child, it would be Theo who would inherit and continue the family business. And so, his parents readily agreed for him to immerse himself into farming life for eighteen months, provided Theo agreed to work abroad for six months once he turned eighteen. His parents were keen for him to see the world before he tied himself to the farm. He was due to leave the week after her father died, and at the time, Jodie couldn't bear the thought of him leaving without sharing her devastating news.

She'd sent him a message to meet her at their usual place, told Kate she was going to meet him, and off she'd gone. Just outside the border of their farm, there was a little cove where the wild seals lived. Seal Cove. It was a sheer cliff face and inaccessible to humans, enabling the seals to live their lives away from human interference. But through the overgrowth was a path, if you knew where to look for it. It was safe enough; Kate would never have taken her there as a child if it wasn't. Twenty yards down the steep path took you to an opening that could not be seen from the cliff top. It was about twelve feet wide and twelve feet deep; perfectly big enough for two people to sit comfortably. And it was here that she and Theo often met to watch the seals play under the setting sun whilst they talked about anything and everything, and he would sing to her.

She did not have to wait long, and as soon as she saw him, she had broken down. In moments he'd wrapped his arms around her and held her whilst she cried into his comforting shoulder...and then, she didn't know how it happened. They were not boyfriend and girlfriend. She adored him completely, and deep down she'd wondered, in time, if they could ever be anything more. But they were so young, and she valued his friendship too much to ever really question if they could ever be more than friends, and he had never hinted towards anything else, so she was content with the friendship that they had. But something changed on the clifftop that evening. One moment he was stroking her hair and muttering soothing words into her ear, and then the next, panic was running through her as they both hastily pulled their clothes back on. An awkwardness had fallen between them then. He was kind, and lovely, and held her hand as they climbed back up the steep path, but neither of them knew what to say to each other on their parting, and after a brief hug, Theo told her that he would call her soon. They had messaged each other frequently, both trying to pretend that nothing had happened by him asking how she was and her asking about his trip, but not once did they mention the elephant in the room.

Jodie stiffened when she saw Kate and Artie return. She flicked the kettle on and arranged the cupcakes on the kitchen table in readiness for Kate's arrival. By the time she'd placed two steaming mugs of tea next to the cupcakes, she heard Kate open the front door and kick off her boots. She waited quietly for Kate to settle herself at the table and initiate the conversation. Jodie noticed she looked calm. Tired and worn out, but calm. And after she'd taken a slurp of her tea, and a bite of her cake, she looked at her.

"So, I obviously have some questions, but firstly, I want to know how you feel about it all. How do you want to go forward with this?"

Jodie knew what she wanted. The question was whether Kate would let her do what she wanted. Her sister was giving her the chance to tell her and so, after taking a deep breath, she explained her plan.

"I want to leave school. I want to help you run our business. Without Dad you can't possibly do everything on your own. Let me help you, Kate."

Kate just looked at her. She said nothing, encouraging her to continue.

"This is as much my farm as it is yours and I want to be a part of it," Jodie continued. "You and Dad have cushioned me from the realities of the financial side of things for so long and what it means to run our farm as a business. It's a family farm, Kate, and I'm part of the family."

"And the baby?" asked Kate.

"Being at home means I could raise the baby and work. I know I won't be able to do any heavy lifting when I get bigger, but it won't be for long. I want this, Kate. You know it's what I always wanted."

"Yes, I know," replied Kate quietly. "Ok then, if you're sure that's what you want, I'll call the school tomorrow."

Jodie relaxed her tensed frame, jumped up from her chair, and wrapped her arms around her sister. "Thank you, Kate."

"Don't thank me yet," she replied with a wry laugh. "There's more to farming and horse training than galloping across the beach and counting the cattle every morning! We can make a list of all the chores and divide them up between us, then we can take it from there."

Jodie couldn't believe how well her sister was taking her news, but she didn't question it. Gratitude swept through her. Kate yet again, had smoothed over a difficult situation that she herself had created.

"So, who's the father?"

Jodie knew it wouldn't be long before Kate broached that subject, and with Kate being so understanding, she knew it would be wrong to deny her sister that information.

"I'll tell you. I don't want any secrets between us, Kate, but you have to promise not to tell anyone because he doesn't know yet, ok?"

Her sister nodded, waiting for her to confide in her.

"It's Theo." And on saying his name out loud, all of her jumbled up feelings and hormonal emotions came pouring out of her. In a split second, Kate's arms were around her, and once her sobbing had subsided, Kate whispered, "I'd better put the kettle on. You can tell me everything, right from the beginning."

Jonah

Jonah and Jonty had idled away the first two weeks of their time together ambling along the Cornish coastal path. He asked nothing from his new horse other than to follow closely alongside him, which he did, uncomplainingly. Sometimes Jonah chatted away to him, and sometimes they walked along in companionable silence enjoying the awe-inspiring coastal views, or quietly watching the wild ponies graze. Jonah and Jonty were enjoying their stroll through Cornwall very much indeed. And as seemed to be the way with Jonah, he happened upon a local farmer in need of a worker for a couple of weeks. They got chatting when Jonah stopped and asked him for directions to the local shop, as he was in need of supplies. It transpired that Farmer Jones's wife had just had their second baby and they were in desperate need of a helping hand until she was back on her feet. As much as Jonah was enjoying his wanderings, the early spring nights were cold in his one-man tent and the thought of a warm bed, and a stable for Jonty, encouraged him to take up the farmer's offer of work.

The work was hard going. The Jones family were sheep farmers and lambing season had just begun. Jonah and Mr Jones rotated shifts around the clock for three solid weeks as lamb after lamb, from their one hundred and fifty ewes, were born. It was exhausting but rewarding work, and a smile never failed to appear on Jonah's face each time a healthy lamb stood up for the first time and suckled its mother. Jonah also dedicated half an hour, every single day, no matter how tired he was, to training Jonty. After the three weeks, Jonah had backed his horse and was riding him confidently bareback in just his halter, using the lead rope as makeshift reins. Jonah accompanied Mr Jones to town in order to purchase Jonty's first saddle, bridle and saddle bag. His time with the Jones family was almost up and he was keen to leave the farm with Jonty being a capable, albeit green, riding horse.

His final week was spent helping Mr Jones with fencing, and any other heavy lifting jobs he could think of that he didn't want his wife doing so soon after giving birth, and then it was time for Jonah to take his leave. Handing over his meagre earnings, the kindly farmer apologised for the low wage, and thanked him profusely for helping him in his time of need. Plus, another nugget of information was given. A local farm, owned by a Mr and Mrs Stevens, about eight miles away, might be in need of a worker. Their only boy was away for a few months and would not be returning until after the harvest.

Jonah put his foot in the stirrup, swung his leg athletically over his horse, and settled into his new saddle. He waved goodbye to Mr and Mrs Jones, then plodded down their drive, inhaled the fresh countryside air, and felt freedom envelop him. Jonah mulled over the information Mr Jones had just given him. His whole being was craving solitude after his busy month, but the thought of a warm bed during the inclement Cornish spring weather also played on his mind.

They reached the crossroads that Mr Jones mentioned in his directions regarding the neighbouring farm. Left would take them to the coastal path, eventually leading them to the farm. Right would take them into town, and straight on would bring them to a large woodland. Jonah contemplated his options.

"Maybe we could head in that general direction?" he asked out loud to his horse. Then he watched Jonty's ears twitch in reply.

"Ok then. We'll go left. Good team talk."

Jonty was proving to be a reliable, trustworthy riding horse. Although green, his natural disposition was calm and steady. The two weeks travelling cross country, and the month immersed in working farm life had opened his eyes up to the world, alongside Jonah's easy going training methods. The big grey horse seemed to take everything in his stride as they plodded along. He even waited patiently when they pulled into a gateway for a tractor and trailer to drive on by.

Jonah guided Jonty off the country lane and on to the track signposted to the costal path. They weaved their way up the overgrown track with Jonah ducking under the low over-hanging tree branches until the path levelled out, and then they were met with the wide-open space of common land and the most spectacular sea view.

"Oh yes, Jonty! This was definitely the right way to come. Look at that view!"

His horse nickered in response.

Jonah and Jonty continued their amble for half an hour, all the while soaking up the stunning surroundings, until Jonah announced it was lunch time. Replacing Jonty's bridle with his head collar, he allowed him to graze whilst he tucked into the homemade sandwich Mrs Jones had made for him. The sky was clear, the sun was shining and bringing with it a little warmth as Jonah gazed across the horizon. Jonty's ears pricked. He lifted his head from his grazing, suddenly alert.

"What is it, boy?"

And then Jonah saw them. A horse and rider galloping flat out across the wide-open common land, with a beautiful collie running along beside them. The horse was jet black, a real black beauty, thought Jonah, not taking his eyes off them. He presumed them to be locals the way they were careering around the undulating ground, the rider carefully directing the horse around the many gorse bushes and hidden ditches, no doubt choosing a well-known path. And then his breath caught in his throat on watching the dog, followed by the powerful black horse, and his talented rider effortlessly clear a stone wall. And without breaking stride, the horse continued to gallop, carrying his rider off into the distance, and out of Jonah's sight.

"Well," said Jonah to his horse, as he slipped off his head collar and replaced it with the bridle. "That's how it's done, my friend. I hope you were paying attention!"

They continued their journey, following the coastal path, just like Mr Jones had instructed. The far-reaching common land finally came to an end, and they followed the narrow path that would lead them to the edge of the farmer's land. Although Mr Jones had advised them to keep going until they reached the beach, then follow the country lanes to the farmhouse and introduce themselves properly. It might not be sensible to ride across someone's private fields without their permission, and he didn't want to make a bad impression before he'd even met the farmer.

Jonah was contemplating where he could pitch his tent for the night, still not having decided whether he was going to go and meet the farmer, when he saw the black horse. He was tied up to a hitching post, and both the rider and dog were nowhere to be seen.

"Maybe we'll just hang back here," he said to Jonty. "Make sure everything is as it should be."

Seeing the riderless horse had unsettled him. He was certain nothing untoward had happened as the horse seemed to have been deliberately tied up. But they were in the middle of nowhere, so just to be on the safe side, and out of loyalty to a fellow rider, he climbed out of his saddle and led his horse back up the track. He positioned himself, he hoped, far enough away to not be seen, but close enough to have a clear view of the horse, and hopefully his rider when they returned.

The minutes slowly ticked by as Jonty grazed and Jonah watched the horse, never taking his eye off him. And then, seemingly out of nowhere, a tall, slim, red-haired woman emerged from the cliff edge through a gorse bush, with the familiar-looking collie at her heels. *Wait a minute, I recognise her from somewhere.* Then he looked at his horse, then back to the woman as she slipped on her riding hat and clipped up the buckle. *The woman from the sales! The one who bid against me for Jonty.*

She was prettier than he remembered. But there was something about her demeanor that told him now was not the time to approach her. She had a weariness about her that she didn't have at the sales. He got the feeling that a sadness was shrouding her and that the only company she was seeking was that of her horse and loyal dog. But after witnessing her fearless riding style on her magnificent horse, Jonah knew that he wanted to see her again.

He watched her elegantly mount her black beauty, walk ten feet down the path, then bend down, unlatch a gate, and expertly manoeuvre her horse to close it behind her, before marching away with her collie skipping along beside her.

Jonah stepped out of his hiding place and walked to the gate she had gone through. It was marked 'private.'

"She must be from around here," he said to Jonty. "Maybe we will go and find Farmer Stevens and see if he has any work going. It might be worth hanging around here for a little while."

Theo

Theo was in his cabin scrolling through the photographs on his phone of Jodie, of which there were many. Pictures of her pulling silly faces, and a cracker of a photo that he'd taken about six months ago when they were drunk in his father's hay barn. A selfie of them both smiling, bleary eyed, into the camera holding up their beer bottles, and then he stopped scrolling when he saw her beautiful face, with her golden ringlets hanging around her shoulders, perfectly matching in colour to Pumpkin's flowing mane, who was standing at her side. Her big blue eyes were filled with surprise, as he caught her unawares when he snapped the photo. She wasn't posing, she wasn't being silly, and his picture had captured the real Jodie with her one true love, Pumpkin. Late at night, sometimes he wondered what it might be like to be Pumpkin. To be showered in adoration and loved unconditionally by Jodie. He knew he was Jodie's best friend - she told him often enough - but deep down he often hoped that one day she would look at him in the same way she looked at her horse.

Theo had loved Jodie since forever. She was the girl next door who he'd grown up with. She wasn't giggly, plastered in make-up and desperate for a boyfriend like all the other girls their age seemed to be. She liked to be at home, on her farm, spending her time baking and cooking delicious treats for her family, and she was always keen to use Theo as her taster if she was trying out a new recipe. And any time away from her kitchen was spent with Pumpkin.

It was his mum who suggested he go away for a while. He didn't know how she knew, but she did. Her motherly instincts, and intuition, told her that he was in love with Jodie. One evening he'd come in from work to find Jodie chatting at the kitchen table with his mother. She'd brought over some peanut butter and chocolate brownies and wanted his opinion on them. The three of them drank tea, munched away on her delicious brownies, and put the world to rights. After Kate called over to collect her, his mother offered him a beer. He'd been surprised at her gesture, but she had stated he would be eighteen soon, all but an adult, and she intended to treat him like one. And then she looked at him softly and told him that she knew. After his initial shock had worn off, he actually found it a relief to finally share his feelings with someone, even if it was his mother. They had talked long into the night and agreed that until Theo knew for sure if Jodie returned his feelings, he should keep them to himself, at least for now. She was just about to turn seventeen, too young for any pressure to be put on her and too young to really know what she wanted. And they were best friends and neighbours. If Theo was rejected, he would still have to live every day of his life next door to her. So, his mother came up with the plan to go away for a while. The distance would make the heart grow fonder, for both of them. Or he would relish in the freedom of travelling for six months, then on his return, be ready to take over the farm and continue the friendship he and Jodie always had, just as it was.

It was because of Jodie he was where he was now. After explaining to her that it had always been the plan his parents insisted upon for him to leave for six months, once he turned eighteen, she relished in the excitement of helping him choose where to go. And during one of their many Google searches, she came across an advert for cruise ship entertainment. A singer was required to entertain the guests in the evenings on board a five-star cruise ship as it sailed around the Mediterranean. It stopped off in various ports for the guests to enjoy the finest aspects of a selection of Mediterranean countries. Jodie had positively bounced up and down with excitement and insisted he applied, and like always, Jodie's excitement was infectious, and he allowed her to carry him away with her idea. He remembered how she had run her hands through his hair, sending shivers down his back, in her attempt to make him look like 'boy band' material for the video she was taking of him playing the guitar and singing.

His dad wasn't happy. The gig started just before lambing season and he would not return until after the harvest, but his mother had been adamant, and like Theo, his father knew that when his mother put her foot down, nothing and no one would change her mind.

A loud knock on his door brought Theo away from his daydreaming about Jodie.

"On stage in five minutes," called out his new friend, James, and fellow entertainer.

Theo, James, and Lynsey shared the stage. They rotated between the kids' club and disco in the afternoon, and the adults' entertainment in the evening. Theo had spent all afternoon with the kids and now had the first hour of the adults' entertainment before he could resume his self-pitying wallowing in the privacy of his cabin.

It was a good crowd, who offered plenty of cheering after each song, and many would sing along with him if they knew the words. When he was playing, he didn't think about Jodie. He lost himself in the music and the distraction of the merry holiday makers before him. The first forty-five minutes were a set list of songs for him to sing, then the last fifteen minutes were available for the guests to make requests, and no matter what it was, if he knew it, he had to sing it. His boss had been very clear about that on day one. It was the guests' holiday, not his, and he was to do everything in his power to make it as enjoyable as possible for them. He felt the pinnacle of his musical career was when an adorable little girl had requested *Let it Go* from the Disney movie *Frozen*. And much to his own dismay, he graciously accepted her request because he knew each and every word.

A woman in the crowd caught his attention and a hush descended as she called out her request.

"Can you do *Perfect* by Ed Sheeran? It's my favourite," she said, beaming up at him, and his heart sank into his boots.

"I'm sorry, I don't know that one, but James does. He's up next so you can ask him then," and before the woman could reply, a man shouted out, "Otis Redding, *Sitting on the Dock of the Bay?*"

"Yes, Sir, coming right up." And he launched into song before any more requests could be made.

He smiled in thanks at the cheering crowd as he introduced James to take over from him, and as soon as was polite to do so, he scarpered back to his cabin. He looked at the photo of Jodie and Pumpkin again and felt a wave of sadness sweep over him. Propping his phone up so he could see her beautiful face, he picked up his guitar and sang *Perfect* by Ed Sheeran to her. It was her favourite song. Their song. He had sung it to her, at her request, at least one hundred times, and he would only sing it for her.

His heart felt heavy, his throat thickened with heat, and his eyes prickled with tears. He'd been away two months, and it had been two months and one week since he'd held her in his arms at Seal Cove. He was overcome with guilt with what he had done, and he could not rid himself the shame of his actions. She'd needed him to support her and to look after her on that harrowing day. Her heart was broken from the sudden loss of her father, and she'd chosen him to seek comfort from during her hour of need. And he wanted to, he had desperately wanted to comfort her, and when she'd first fallen into his arms and cried her heart out on his shoulder, his only desire was to hold her.

But then she kissed me. No, I kissed her. I don't know who kissed who first, he thought, desperately trying to remember when things changed from him holding her sobbing frame in his arms to passionately kissing each other. *I should have stopped. I shouldn't have let it happen. I took advantage of her when she was vulnerable. But I didn't stop, and neither did she.* And he definitely remembered her saying not to stop, but that wasn't the point. He should never have let it happen. Afterwards, he'd wanted to tell her there and then that he was in love with her. That he'd always been in love with her. But he knew it wasn't the right time and that it would have been selfish of him. She was confused, and angry and hurting about her father, and for him to spring his undying love on her would have been unfair. Instead, he hugged her awkwardly, as close to him as he dared, then walked away.

And now he was lord knows how many hundreds of miles away from her, not knowing how she was or how she really felt, because no doubt just like him, she was avoiding the whole situation by not bringing it up, or even hinting at in in their messages at all. Not even his mother could fix this sorry mess for him, and he cringed with shame at the thought of his loyal, wonderful mum finding out what he'd done, even after she'd organised the perfect get-out clause for him. She'd argued with his father on his behalf that the cruise ship was the best thing for him, even though it meant going away for the duration of the harvest instead of the original plan of Theo going away through the autumn and winter months. She'd fought his corner and supported him every step of the way. Theo could not bear the utter disappointment she would feel in him if she were ever to find out the truth...and God forbid if Kate ever found out. He'd seen her in full blown fury when he and Jodie were about eight or nine years old. They'd taken themselves off for a picnic with their ponies, but not told anyone where they were going. And it was safe to say that after Kate had got hold of them, they had never disappeared without telling her again. He thought his mum got cross, but blimey, she didn't have a patch on Kate once she was riled up.

The utter chaos he'd got himself into went round and round his head. He couldn't escape it, and in all honesty, he didn't want to. He deserved the shame and guilt. And the disgrace that he would bring on his family if they ever found out. But what kept him awake into the long twilight hours the most was wondering if Jodie would ever forgive him. And would she ever love him the way he loved her? Or had he ruined it for himself, maybe for them both, before anything had even begun?

Kate

Kate was on the yard tacking up Pumpkin. Both she and Jodie had decided from the get-go that Jodie would not ride for the duration of her pregnancy. It wasn't worth the risk, no matter how much she trusted Pumpkin. Kate looked over Pumpkin and into the paddock where her sister was schooling Charlie, and she had to admit, over the past five weeks, Jodie had been as good as her word. She was up and out as soon as her morning sickness had subsided, feeding the horses, mucking out and helping Kate to train the auction horses, Philippa and Charlie. Jodie appeared to be as dedicated to the horses as Kate herself was. And as she watched her, she could see that Jodie was steadily becoming a capable horse trainer.

It also transpired that Jodie was a whizz at maths. She'd got her head around their accounting system fairly quickly, and they were now at the point where Kate could leave her to get on with it in the afternoons whilst she spent her time outdoors, just where she like to be, working on the farm. And when Kate came home in the evenings, a home-cooked, delicious meal was always waiting for her, in a welcoming, clean home.

Kate mounted Pumpkin, waved goodbye to Jodie, then plodded down their drive for a quick ride around the lanes, with Flo at her heels, before her afternoon check of their twenty-three cows with their twenty-three healthy calves at foot. Pumpkin clip-clopped along the lane and Kate inhaled the sweet flowery fragrance from the pretty hedgerow flowers that were dancing delicately in the breeze. For Kate, there was nowhere more beautiful than Cornwall in springtime. They passed the entrance to Theo's family farm and Kate thought back to how she had wanted to throttle the little bastard as soon as she found out what he'd done. But then it was Jodie who reminded her that Theo was yet to find out exactly what he had done. Even so, Kate had quietly fumed. He should never have put them both in the position where Jodie could get pregnant in the first place. But now, although she could never be truly happy about her sister's situation, she was at least beginning to see the silver lining from it all. She even admitted to herself that as far as boys were concerned, Theo was a nice one. He adored Jodie, he was always reliable and dropped her home when he said he would, not to mention that his family farmed next door and both families had known each other forever... Although who knew how his parents would react when they find out their eighteen-year-old son is about to become a father, Kate thought wryly.

Morning sickness aside, she'd never seen Jodie so contented. She knew that her father had been doing his best, trying to do the right thing by Jodie by making her stay in school, and truth be told, Kate had whole heartedly agreed with him. But he was no longer here. When Kate went out riding, galloping for miles across the common land near the farm the day she found out Jodie was pregnant, she resigned herself to the fact that Jodie must make her own decisions. If she was old enough to have a baby, she was old enough to decide the direction of her future. So, Kate had let her decide her own fate, and it seemed that Jodie knew what was best for Jodie, because as far as Kate could tell, she was thriving.

The other silver lining to the pregnancy was the distraction from their grief. They grieved, of course, sometimes together, sometimes alone, and often with their horses, but with a baby due in just over six months, there was plenty to be done and lots to look forward too. And the next big date marked on their calendar was Jodie's twelve week scan the following week, Kate couldn't wait. She'd even caught herself looking at a teeny tiny t-shirt with a pony on it at the local tack store, thinking how much Jodie would like it and how cute it would look on her little niece or nephew.

She felt a raindrop land on her hand and looked up. The ever-changing Cornish weather had brought dark clouds over head which were now hiding the weak spring sunshine. She checked her watch.

"Enough dawdling!" she said to Pumpkin, as she pushed her into trot for the last leg of the journey home. It was getting late, and she had work to do.

Kate hurried through her chores as fast as she dared to go. The looming dark clouds were staying put and the persistent drizzle was fast turning into a heavy downpour. When all animals were fed, and she had confirmed that they were all where they should be, she tumbled through her front door just as the first rumble of thunder broke loose.

"It's going to be a corker of a storm tonight!" she called out to Jodie.

"I know, I know," replied Jodie, hurrying to dry Flo with a towel before she shook her soggy, wet furry self all over the house.

"Run upstairs and have a hot shower to warm up. I've lit the fire; we'll eat in the sitting room tonight."

Kate did as instructed. Then in her fleecy pyjamas, with her wet hair wrapped in a towel on her head, she padded back downstairs and into the cosy sitting room. The log fire was roaring, and Flo was stretched out drying herself on the fireside rug. As soon as she settled herself on their big, squishy sofa, Jodie came bustling in laden with hot bowls of vegetable soup and home-made crusty rolls, dripping in butter. Kate's mouth watered just looking at it.

"You are the best!" she said to her sister, meaning every word. She'd never been looked after quite so well since Jodie had taken over the house and cooking chores.

Just as the sisters were tucking into warm apple pie, with a generous dollop of clotted cream on top, Kate's phone rang, and Kate saw Mr Stevens' name flash up on her screen. She and Jodie had been avoiding Mr and Mrs Stevens. They were polite if they saw them out and about, but they did not seek them out deliberately, for fear of letting slip of Jodie's pregnancy. And as guilty as they felt about allowing people to think they were keeping themselves to themselves whilst they were grieving their father, they did nothing to make people believe anything else.

"Hello, Mr Stevens," answered Kate.

"Kate, I'm so sorry to call you at such a ghastly hour, but I've got a bit of an emergency on my hands," said Mr Stevens.

"Is Mrs Stevens ok?" replied Kate, crossing her fingers that her lovely, warm friendly neighbour was not hurt in any way, and mentally telling herself off for avoiding them for such a long time.

"Yes, yes, she's fine. Twenty young ewes, with their lambs at foot, have spooked in the storm and got themselves lost on the common land. If it was just the ewes, I wouldn't worry so much, but the lambs will never survive a storm like this up there. There's no one who knows every nook and cranny of that land like you do. Is there any chance you could help?" pleaded Mr Stevens.

"Of course. I'll bring Flo. And Artie?" Kate thought that she could cover a lot more ground on her horse than on foot.

"Yes, bring Artie. I'm going to saddle up my horse now. See you on my yard in fifteen minutes?"

"I'll be there. Goodbye, Mr Stevens." Kate looked longingly at the cosy fireplace that she would now be leaving, and then she looked through the window to see the rain relentlessly pelting against the glass.

"Come along then Flo, we've got work to do." And as Flo stretched and yawned to wake herself up, Kate reiterated to Jodie all that Mr Stevens had told her.

Bundled up into her wet weather gear, with her pyjamas on underneath, Kate and Flo set off along the country lanes to Mr Stevens' farm. Kate had strapped a head torch to her riding hat and after putting Flo in her florescent, waterproof dog coat, she secured a torch to her collar, but the two torches had little effect against the gales force winds and driving rain that they were up against. As much as Kate wished she was back at home with Jodie, she knew she could never leave a fellow farmer in need, and one day, she knew without doubt, that when it was her time in need, the Stevens would return the favour.

Mr Stevens and his horse were waiting for her on his yard. He wasted no time with small talk or pleasantries.

"I've sent my man on ahead of us." Then he thrust a radio into her hands. "In this weather there's no guarantee mobile phones will work. Best to communicate with these. You ready?"

"Yes," she simply replied.

Mr Stevens whistled for his dog, and with Flo running alongside her and Artie, they cantered along the farm track, across two fields, and then they were on the far-reaching common moor land. The wind howled with more ferociousness without trees and hedges to slow its path on the wide-open space of ground, and with the rain pelting them, seemingly from every direction, Kate could barely hear a thing up there.

She parted from Mr Stevens, both knowing they could cover more ground if the split up, so she, Artie and Flo headed into the inky blackness of the night alone. She headed south where she knew there was a large clump of gorse bushes rooted up against an old tumbled down wall which the sheep might have found some shelter under. Riding with her head down, trusting her instincts and the capability and loyalty of her animal companions, they marched against the driving wind. All the while she was hoping and praying that the little lambs, wherever they were, would survive this horrendous storm.

Kate could have wept when she found the gorse bush empty of any sheep. She sent Flo around to circle the bushes again, to double check they hadn't missed anything, but they were not there. She pondered momentarily as to where to set off next when her radio crackled. An unfamiliar voice announced he had found all but one ewe and lamb. He was driving them west to the border of Mr Stevens' farmland.

Kate, Artie, and Flo cautiously but purposefully retraced their steps. She saw a figure ahead; she had no idea if it was Mr Stevens or his man, but whoever it was, they were slowly but surely pushing the sheep over the rugged common land.

"I'm here, I can see the ewes," Kate shouted through the radio.

"Can you push them home?" replied the man. "I need to go back, we're one short."

Before Kate had time to answer, Mr Stevens crackled through. "You carry on, Jonah. Kate and I can drive them home."

Although the storm continued to rage around them, Kate, Artie, and Flo got to work. Flo excelled herself, working alongside Mr Stevens' sheep dog, helping to keep the sheep moving as one, and pushing along any stragglers. Both horses and riders and dogs, worked together to guide the sheep across Mr Stevens' fields, down his track, until finally, they scampered into his dry barn.

And just as they secured the latch on the gate, Jonah's voice crackled through the radio. "I've found her, we'll be down in ten minutes."

Mr Stevens let out a heavy sigh of relief, then looked at Kate. "Thank you, thank you for all your help. After this, I owe you big time!" he said sincerely.

"Any time, Mr Stevens. That's what neighbours are for!" she laughed in reply.

Kate was soaked, right through to her bare skin, and with the adrenaline slowly winding down now that the work was done, she felt shivers through her body, and all she could think about was her cosy sitting room and a second helping of apple pie. As if reading her thoughts, Mr Stevens, ushered her to get home. He and Jonah could manage by themselves now.

The relentless storm still raged as she pushed Artie into a forward-going trot home along the country lanes. Her warm house and pudding were waiting for her.

Jodie

Jodie was lying down on the hospital bed with her hand firmly clasped in Kate's. The friendly sonographer was bustling around them getting everything prepared for her much anticipated twelve-week scan.

"Ok then, Jodie, are we ready to see your baby?" the sonographer asked, and after acknowledging Jodie's' nod, she tucked her shirt up and squelched the ultrasound gel onto her belly.

Moments later she heard it. The rapid beat of her baby's heartbeat ringing out loud and clear in the quiet hospital room. Then the sonographer traced her finger on the computer screen showing them both the outline of her baby. She looked at Kate, but Kate did not return her look. She was staring open mouthed at the screen, drinking in every detail of her little niece or nephew.

Seeing her baby on the screen made it all feel so real. She was going to have a baby. Her very own baby. She couldn't wait! A family was all she ever wanted. She had often pictured it, her brood of children toddling around the farmyard, she and Kate teaching them how to ride their ponies and baking all their favourite treats to her heart's content in her cosy farmhouse kitchen. *A little earlier than planned*, she thought ruefully, *but I can't change that now!* Her dream was slowly becoming a reality, and although the matter of the baby's father hadn't quite been ironed out yet, she had Kate. And with Kate by her side, she knew that all would be well.

"You have a very healthy baby," beamed the sonographer, "and it looks like he or she should be arriving on or near the twentieth of December."

"A Christmas baby!" squeaked Kate.

"A Christmas baby," echoed Jodie, counting down the months on her fingers. "Six whole months," she said out loud. "It seems forever away!"

Kate and the sonographer burst out laughing at her impatience.

"We've got lots to organise before baby comes along," smiled Kate.

Jodie and Kate were discussing potential baby names when they turned into their farm driveway and saw a man sitting astride his horse on their yard. He smiled and waved on seeing them, and by the time Kate had pulled up the Land Rover, he had dismounted from his horse in readiness to greet them.

"Kate and Jodie?" he asked.

"That's right, I'm Jodie," she introduced herself, all the while wondering who the handsome stranger was and his equally handsome horse.

"And you are?" she asked, holding out her hand to cement their introduction.

"Jonah, I'm working for Mr Stevens next door."

Jodie turned to Kate, who was yet to utter a single word. She was staring intently at his horse. Jodie nudged her sister gently, wondering why she seemed to have completely forgotten her manners.

"You've got my horse!" Kate suddenly blurted out.

"Urrrrm," said Jonah, "I think he's my horse!"

"Sorry, yes of course," stammered Kate. "I meant the horse I wanted. I'd recognise him anywhere." She pointed to the inky black half-moon marking. "You were the one who out bid me at the sales!"

"Guilty, I'm afraid," replied Jonah.

As he flicked his tousled black locks out of his face, Jodie thought again, how positively gorgeous he was. Ancient of course, he had to be at least thirty, but still, proper fit for an oldie!

"I recognise you, though," Jonah continued, "from the sales, and I've seen you riding out and about whilst I've been working at the Stevens' farm, which reminds me, that's why I'm here. I'm to invite you to dinner this evening, both of you, as a thank you from Mr and Mrs Stevens for your help the other night."

"We'd love too," Jodie chipped in before her sister could come up with an excuse to say no. And she did want to go. It had been months since she'd seen Theo's parents, and no matter how much she didn't like to think about it, they would always be the grandparents of her baby.

Jodie watched Jonah flick his eyes over to her, offer a quick smile, then his attention was back to Kate, who apparently had nothing to say.

"Mrs Stevens said seven o'clock," said Jonah as he mounted his handsome grey gelding.

"We'll be there," Jodie called out as he trotted down their drive. Then she turned to Kate. "Ok, before you get cross with me, I've been thinking. If we keep avoiding them for ever, they're going to get suspicious. I'm not showing yet so I'm thinking it's better to see them now, smooth things over and act like everything is fine before they start knocking on our door trying to be neighbourly only to find me the size of a whale. Then we really would have some explaining to do."

Jodie watched her sister mull over her reasoning and to her relief, she saw her frown melt away before she replied, "I hadn't thought of it like that. You're right. We have to go."

"Good, that's settled. Now," she said with a little smirk on her face, "I hope you're going to make an effort. That hot cowboy couldn't take his eyes off you!"

"Jodie!" Kate chased her into the house, teasing her, just like she used to do before their father died. And Jodie thought it felt nice to have a little bit of normality back, and to hear Kate laugh. Her sister had been under so much pressure after losing their father and having to step up and take charge of both businesses, not to mention Jodie's unexpected situation that she'd dumped on her. *Yes*, thought Jodie, *it's about time Kate let her hair down and had a little fun.*

Overall, Jodie was pleased with her sister's appearance. Kate was never one for dressing up, but at least she'd put on a pair of skinny jeans that showed off her slim, long legs, and her navy-blue fitted shirt with daisies on it. Jodie was also wearing jeans with a floaty floral shirt which showed off her favourite necklace. Theo had given it to her for her seventeenth birthday and she knew his mum would recognise it, and that would be another indication that all was well between them. She gently fingered the turquoise pendant and thought of Theo. Truth be told, she did little else. He was always at the forefront of her mind, and in her daydreams, he was as equally happy as she was about starting a family together. And every single day her heart skipped a beat when her phone beeped, and she saw that it was a message from him. But tonight wasn't about her, it was about Kate. An evening for her to relax with friends and... *well*, she thought, *let's see if any sparks fly between Kate and the neighbour's hot cowboy!*

Jodie and Kate were both welcomed with open arms by Mrs Stevens. She was a cuddly lady, just how Jodie imagined a mother should be. Growing up she'd always held a little envy of Theo that he still had his mum, and a lovely one at that. She must have spent half of her life at his house and his mum had never made her feel like she'd overstayed her welcome, quite the opposite in fact. Many a time she had told Jodie how much she enjoyed her company, and that she got a lot more sense and interesting conversation out of her than the two men she lived with!

The sisters were ushered into the Stevens' dining room and even though Jodie had been in there many times without Theo, this time she felt the lack of his presence greatly. And guilt filtered through her at the huge secret she was carrying, and anxiety swept through her that things would never be the same again once everyone found out the truth. And that maybe Theo didn't love her like she loved him. That was the one thing she was now sure of, and when she thought about it, she realised that she'd always been in love with him. She just hadn't allowed herself to acknowledge those feelings for fear of being rejected and losing her best friend. To have Theo as her best friend was better than not having him at all. But she was not the same innocent teenager anymore. She was going to be the mother of Theo's child and over the past few weeks she'd forced herself to face the feelings she had buried for so long, and finally admit the truth. She loved him, it was as simple as that. And she did not regret their time together at Seal Cove cliff top, not one bit.

She felt Kate put her arm around her. "Are you ok?" she whispered. "We can go if it's all too much for you."

Jodie appreciated her sister's astuteness at her change in mood, and then she reminded herself why they were here. For Kate. And right on cue, Jonah walked in. This time he was clean-shaven, his still damp hair was slicked back, and he was wearing dark denim jeans with a light blue shirt. *Oooooh hello!* thought Jodie, and all thoughts of her own love life were pushed firmly to the back of her mind. *You will definitely do for my sister!*

The conversation flowed easily around the dinner table and Mrs Stevens had positively outdone herself with the feast she provided for them. Roast lamb, from their own home-bred flock, with all the trimmings, followed by raspberry pavlova. Jodie and Mrs Stevens were deep in conversation about how to make the perfect meringue when Mr Stevens called everyone to attention.

"Kate, I just wanted to formally say thank you so much for your help last week. Jonah and I honestly couldn't have done it without you. The weather was utterly horrendous, the job ahead of us was ghastly, and not once did you stop and think about what you were getting into. You just jumped on that horse of yours and came to our rescue. Mrs Stevens and I just wanted you to know how much we appreciate you."

Jodie watched her sister colour with embarrassment at being put into the centre of attention and receiving such high praise, and she felt for her. Kate didn't do public displays of affection. But she was also secretly pleased that Kate's kindness and tireless work ethic was earning her the credit she so deserved. And she also noticed that Jonah did not take his eyes off Kate for the duration of Mr Stevens' heartfelt speech.

"So," continued Mr Stevens, "If there is ever anything that you girls need, or any emergency that you need help with, then you must always know that we will be there at the drop of a hat. And don't hesitate to call on us. Just because Theo is away, it doesn't mean that we aren't here for you girls. Your father was a dear friend of ours and we farmers look out for one another."

Kate smiled and thanked Mr and Mrs Stevens politely, but Jodie knew that she would not call on the help of anyone unless it was truly a full-scale emergency. Jodie, however, didn't see the harm in asking for help if she needed it, and she could feel a plan forming.

"Actually Mr Stevens, now that you mention it, there is something that you might be able to help me with." She didn't dare look at Kate. She could feel her sister's eyes boring into her and knew she'd be in for a telling off later, but hopefully it would all be worth it in the end.

"What is it, Jodie?" asked Mr Stevens eagerly.

"Well, last year Mr Fox murdered all of my chickens, and Dad said he'd fix my chicken coop, but..."

She let her words trail off and hoped that she wouldn't go to hell for the blatant use of her dead father to kick-start her plan. And technically, she justified to herself, it is true. Dad did say he would fix it for me.

"Of course, no problem, I can get that fixed for you," said Mr Stevens. "In fact, Jonah, maybe you could pop over next week? Jodie can show you what needs to be done and you can get an idea of the materials we'll need."

"Of course, Mr Stevens," replied Jonah.

Bingo! Aloud, Jodie simply said, "Thanks, that would be great."

Jonah

Jonah was tucking into his full English breakfast at the Stevens' breakfast table, just like he did every morning. He'd well and truly landed on his feet working for them. It transpired that Farmer Jones had called ahead on the chance that Jonah would take his advice and search out the Stevens. The kind man had sung his praises and told Mr Stevens that he would happily vouch for him if needed. And Mr Stevens was in a bit of a bind. The local man who was due to start work for the six months whilst his son, Theo, was away, went and broke his leg on a drunken night out, right in the middle of lambing season. Mr Stevens had been furious, and once meeting Jonah for himself, he'd hired him on the spot. The Stevens' farm was a much larger operation than the friendly, albeit tumbling down Jones' farm. Mr Stevens owned five hundred acres, and with it, three hundred ewes, one hundred cows with calves at foot, plus one hundred store cattle. His workload was heavy, but he enjoyed it. Mr Stevens paid him well and he was an honest, kind man. Mrs Stevens fussed and mothered him, looking after him as if he was part of the family, so all in all, Jonah was content to stay put until the end of the harvest.

And then there was the matter of the beautiful red-headed woman who lived next door. He'd learned early on about the recent tragedy of the sisters losing their father, coupled with the devastating loss of their mother when they were young. He'd deliberately stayed away to give them the privacy they so obviously needed and wanted. He'd been awed again with Kate's work ethic and horsemanship skills when she'd joined the search for the lost sheep during that horrendous storm, and he knew from his own experiences that she had the utmost respect and loyalty from her animals for them to follow her so willingly on a night like that. Only the most honest and kind-hearted people were capable of forming relationships with animals like that. Animals had a knack for knowing who was good and who was bad, and Jonah could tell that Kate was most definitely one of the good ones. He'd been bowled over when he saw her last week at the Stevens' dinner table. His initial thought was that she scrubbed up well, but after spending an evening in her company, he found her to be so much more than a pretty girl. She talked business with Mr Stevens, and she knew everything there was to know about running her own farm, on top of managing her own horse training business. Not to mention the responsibility of her little sister. And when Mrs Stevens had replaced the lights with candles for after dinner coffee and biscuits, in the warm glow of the flickering flames, Jonah had struggled to take his eyes off her. She'd worn her wild red hair loose around her shoulders, and her green eyes sparkled when she talked about horses with Mr Stevens, and for Jonah, in that very moment, he didn't think he had ever seen anyone quite so beautiful before.

Mrs Stevens placed a carrier bag in front of him.

"A leg of lamb and a dozen fresh eggs for the girls," she announced. "Although after you've fixed the hen house, they should have plenty of their own!"

"I'll make sure Jonty keeps to a steady pace; no eggs will be damaged in transport!" replied Jonah.

Mr Stevens looked up from his *Farmers Weekly* magazine. "Be sure to note if anything else over there needs fixing. Kate would never ask, but since Jodie's asked you to look at the hen house, you might as well see if there is anything else we can do to help them."

"Of course, I'll let you know of anything when I get back this evening," replied Jonah, equally keen to find reasons to visit the neighbouring farm and see Kate again.

"I wouldn't worry so much if our Theo was here, he's always popping over there. Got a soft spot for Jodie, wouldn't you say, Mrs Stevens?"

"Close friends for sure," she chipped in, and if Jonah wasn't mistaken, he sensed a glimmer of unease from her. And then it vanished.

And Mr Stevens continued, "It was a terrible tragedy with regards to their father. Salt of the earth he was, and that Kate is like him in every way."

"I'll keep an eye on them until Theo gets back, don't you worry," replied Jonah.

Jonah directed Jonty down the drive of the girls' farm, and he could see Kate schooling the filly she bought at the sales. He watched her float in circles around Kate as she worked her in a forward-going trot. The horse noticed him and Jonty, pricking her ears briefly to acknowledge their arrival before turning her focus back to Kate, and right on cue, she transitioned up to an elegant rocking horse canter. Not once did Kate look away from the horse.

Jodie, however, came racing out of the house as soon as he arrived.

"You're here, you're here! Welcome!" she called out, then handed him a steaming mug of tea and gave half an apple to Jonty.

Jodie accepted Mrs Stevens' offerings keenly, then said, "once Kate's finished with Philippa, she'll turn Jonty out in that paddock for you." Then she skipped along a little path at the side of her house, gesturing for him to follow her.

Jodie was easy to like. The sisters appeared to be different in every possibly way. Red-headed, pale skinned Kate was tall, slim, reserved in nature and perfectly happy in her own company, and that of her animals. Jodie, on the other hand, was petite, curvy, and bubbly. Jonah noticed she was a very pretty girl, and her golden ringlets bobbed around her shoulders as she chatted and laughed. He was beginning to realise why the illustrious Theo spent so much of his time here and how a teenage boy might so easily fall for Jodie's warmth and friendliness.

Ten minutes later he and Jodie were discussing the hen house when Kate appeared. "I've put Jonty in the paddock," announced Kate.

"Great, thank you," he replied, before turning his attention back to Jodie, trying to work out how the tumble down, rotted wooden ensemble in front them was once a functioning hen house.

"I don't remember it being quite this bad," Jodie explained. "It must have collapsed to its death during the storm."

"Well," said Kate, "now you know what you're up against, I'll let you two get on." And before Jonah had a chance to reply, she'd strolled off back to the horses.

"Oh, don't mind her," said Jodie. "She thinks chickens are just another responsibility, even though for as long as I can remember, it was always me who looked after them, not her. So, I don't know why she's being so grumpy!"

Jonah was secretly pleased that he would be building the hen house from scratch. His time at the sisters' farm would not be an afternoon's patch-up job, but a good few days' work.

Jodie looked up at him, then back to the dilapidated coop anxiously. "Do you think you can fix it?"

"I think I if we can clear all of this away, I can build you a new one."

"Really! Wow, fantastic," she replied eagerly. "Let's get started!"

She advised they move the rotted wood to the other side of the yard where it would be safe to burn later. Between them, they manoeuvred a particularly large panel of wood along the narrow path. As soon as they set foot on the yard, he heard Kate shouting.

"Jodie, put that down right now. You know you're not to lift anything heavy."

And she came racing over to chastise Jodie. Jonah was slightly taken aback with Kate's outburst, but Jodie immediately did as she was told, then announced she would go and make a start on lunch, and after a brief smile to Jonah, she was gone.

"Sorry," Kate mumbled. "She has a bad back. I'll help you."

Jonah and Kate quietly moved all the rotted wood. He was desperate to talk to her, about anything, but he feared that she would shoot him down no matter what topic he chose, and so he remained silent. She looked pale, and tired. Not physically tired; it was more like a weariness about her that she tried to hide.

When the site was cleared, he told Kate that he would borrow Mr Stevens' pickup and go into town and get the materials he would need. He would return tomorrow to start the work.

He saw her face soften. "Thank you, this means a lot to Jodie. She loves chickens! She was completely devastated when the fox got them. I've been meaning to get another coop sorted for ages, but there always seems to be a more pressing job to be done. I really appreciate your help."

"No problem, and if there is anything else you need fixing, just let me know," he replied, with a tentative smile, privately thinking that he wasn't doing it for Jodie, but for her.

"Sorry about before, I've just got a lot on at the moment," she said, with a sweeping gesture of her hand around the horse yard and farm.

Jonah just nodded, hoping that if he remained quiet, she might continue.

"Don't get me wrong, Jodie does her fair share, but..." She faltered, seemingly lost for words momentarily. At last, she continued, "Like I said, she has a bad back so she can't do any of the heavy lifting. Charlie, the other horse I bought at the sales, he went to his new owner yesterday so I should have a bit more time to get through my backlog of jobs." And then she smiled at him, but it didn't quite reach her eyes. Jonah had the suspicious feeling that Kate wasn't telling him the whole story.

"I'd better get going," she announced, putting an end to their conversation, "I've got to exercise Pumpkin." After giving Jonty a quick stroke, she headed off to the tack room.

Jonah lifted his saddle onto Jonty, all the while wondering why Kate, who seemed to have one hundred and one jobs to do, was going to exercise her sister's horse for her, when Jodie was in the house making lunch. He wasn't one for prying. Like Kate, he chose to keep himself to himself. But he hoped that during his time making the chicken coop, he might be able to unravel at least part of the mystery that was going on with the sisters.

Kate

Kate was sitting in the middle of the cow field, holding the head of her father's favourite cow in her arms, sobbing uncontrollably at the unfairness of life. She was an old girl, about fifteen, and Kate had known that this year's calf would most likely be her last. But when she'd seen her healthy, new-born heifer the morning after her father's death, she'd felt a momentary surge of gratitude that the old girl had successfully delivered another calf. But on this summer's morning, under blue skies and sunshine, she had found her dead in the field, and her little heifer was not yet weaned.

Frustration swelled within her. It didn't matter how hard she worked, she was forever taking one step forward, then one step back. And her pain ran deep with the fact she had no one to share it all with. She couldn't risk giving Jodie any added stress with her pregnancy, and truth be told, it was always her dad she'd talked too. Jodie had Theo – the two of them were thick as thieves - and she'd had her dad. After school most of her girlfriends had drifted away, seeking more in life than their little farming community. Kate hadn't been bothered in the slightest. She was more than content to run her business and be her father's right-hand woman. But with him gone, she had no one. And it was at times like this when she struggled to dig deep and find the determination to keep going, that she found his loss almost too much to bear.

Flo licked her nose, anxious at the obvious distress of her mistress. Kate pulled her dog in close, and holding her tightly, let her tears flow into her warm, comforting fur.

The sound of hooves thundering from behind drew her attention away from her heartache, and she saw Jonah and Jonty cantering across the field towards her. She was beginning to get used to Jonah. Initially, she'd been furious with Jodie. What if he found out she was pregnant? What if he told Mr and Mrs Stevens? But Jodie had simply said they would take each day at a time, and surely his help was better than no help at all. And so, he'd become part of the furniture for the time it took him to build Jodie's coop, and then he'd turned up to fix a damaged stable door. Then again to fix some fencing. He was unobtrusive. He never asked nosy questions, he just simply got on with whatever he came over to do. She knew he discussed with Jodie anything that he noticed needing to be done because she always agreed for him to fix it. But Kate appreciated his help, even if she didn't say as much out loud, and eventually decided to let Jodie and Jonah get on with it. What they were going to do when Jodie got bigger, she didn't know. At the moment she just looked like she'd put weight on, but it wouldn't be long before people worked out that she had in fact not eaten all the pies, but that she was pregnant.

"Kate, are you hurt?" Jonah called out. "Is the cow, is she…" His words hung in the air.

"Dead. Yes." Kate sniffed and hastily tried to dry her eyes., "I'm fine."

"No, you're not," Jonah said quietly. "I'll call Mr Stevens." Then he pulled out his phone and had a brief hushed conversation with him.

She tried her hardest but could not quell her tears, and with Jonah crouched in the grass next to her, they continued to flow silently down her cheeks.

"Come on Kate, you can't stay here. Mr Stevens is on his way. He'll move her and put the calf in the stables. You shouldn't be here when he does it. It's not nice for anyone, especially when it's one of your own."

Kate nodded, then felt his strong arms gently slip behind her and lift her to her feet.

"You need to get away from here for an hour. Would you like to borrow Jonty?"

She shook her head in response to his kind gesture.

"Would you like to be on your own?"

And again, she shook her head, because she didn't want to be on her own. Instead, she walked towards the clifftop, gesturing for Jonah to follow.

He followed quietly beside her, leading Jonty, and did not question where they were going. They continued to walk in silence, with loyal little Flo trotting along at Kate's side until they reached the hitching post at the top of Seal Cove.

"You can tie Jonty there," she said. Then she allowed him to follow her through the gorse bushes, down the narrow path, to hers and Jodie's secret place. She knew Theo was in on the secret too - how could he not be being Jodie's best friend? But they had agreed amongst themselves that they would tell no one else. All it took was for one person to blab and it would no longer be theirs. But Jonah was quiet, and private, just like she was, and somehow, she knew that he would never betray their special place to anyone.

"Wow," Jonah said quietly, when they were sitting down looking out to the spectacular sea view before them.

They sat in silence, watching the seals, some dipping and diving in the ocean and others basking in the sunshine on the seashore.

Kate loved the peacefulness that her secret hidey-hole gave her. And she appreciated Jonah's silence whilst she gathered her thoughts and emotions together.

"This is where we scattered their ashes," she started. "I always liked the idea of them being carried away in the breeze. That they weren't constrained like being buried in the ground. They are free, out in the open air, just how they liked to be when they were here."

"I like that idea," replied Jonah.

And then Kate realised that she actually knew very little about the man sitting next to her. She spent so much of her time hiding her own secrets that she had never bothered to find out anything about him, and he had not volunteered any information himself.

"Are you close to your parents?" she asked, hoping that she wouldn't be seen as prying too much into this private man's world.

"Actually, I'm an orphan too," he replied, in a soft but matter of fact tone.

"Oh Jonah, I'm so sorry," she gushed.

"Don't be. Life is what it is. I grew up in foster homes," he stated simply.

Kate noted it was a statement, rather than an invitation to ask more questions, so she said nothing, merely acknowledging that life was always hard no matter who you were or what background you came from. Life would consistently deliver both good times and bad, and all anyone could do was carry on. She closed her eyes and relaxed under the warmth of the summer sun, listening to the gentle waves lapping on the shore down below.

"We'd better get back," Kate announced. "I need to bottle feed that heifer calf."

"I'll help you," Jonah replied. And for the first time, Kate didn't dismiss his offer.

Kate found herself feeling lighter on the walk back to the farm. *Maybe a good cry is what I needed*, Kate thought. Kate had always struggled with her emotions, preferring to keep them to herself, but her dad always knew what was going on, no matter how much she tried to hide her inner feelings. And he always knew what to do. Sometimes he would just put his arm around her and tell her everything would sort itself out in the end. Other times, he'd tack Artie up, hand over his reins and insist she go riding. He never pushed, he never asked, he was just there for her. Without him, she'd feared that no one would ever understand her reserved ways, and that had weighed heavily on her since his passing. That she was truly alone in the world. But Jonah had known. She didn't know how, or why, but he'd behaved just as her father would have done in that situation. He was kind and patient, and offered her the option of solitude with Jonty or his quiet, unobtrusive company. Kate was glad she had chosen to be with him, and whilst sitting on the cliff top, with the warm breeze in her hair, she'd wondered what it might have felt like for him to put his arm around her in comfort. She was relieved he didn't, but that didn't stop the thoughts whirling round her mind that she might have liked it.

The heifer calf drank greedily from the bottle, proving that she was as strong and robust as Kate hoped her to be. And her little old pony, Cupcake, snuffled her and mothered her when she brought her into the stable for company. Leaning on the stable door, Kate and Jonah watched the new little family of two bond.

"Kate! There you are. I've been looking all over for you. Mr Stevens told me what happened when he collected the cow," said a very anxious looking Jodie.

"I'm just settling the calf with Cupcake, then I'll take Pumpkin out for you," Kate said, and she received a beaming smile from Jodie.

"Thanks, you're the best! Better get back, I've got chicken and ham pie in the oven for you! Bye Jonah." And she scurried off back to the kitchen.

"Why doesn't Jodie ride Pumpkin herself?" asked Jonah. And Kate knew he wasn't trying to pry. No doubt he was just confused by the whole situation. It was a perfectly logical question to ask seeing as Jodie was positively horse mad and part of her job was training horses, and as far as anyone could tell, she was a fighting fit seventeen-year-old.

"It's her back, like I told you the other day, but hopefully she'll be back riding soon," Kate said, without making eye contact. The more she got to know Jonah, the more she was beginning to feel uncomfortable telling him fibs.

"You have to exercise all the horses yourself until she gets better? On top of everything else?"

"That's about the size of it," she said lightly, trying to move on from the minefield of a subject. "Pumpkin first, then little Philippa needs a good run. I'd better get to it." And she meant it. She'd wasted enough time being emotional over the cow, and as much as she'd enjoyed her time on the cliff top, there was work to be done.

"Pumpkin's big enough to carry me, why don't I ride her? That way you can get both horses exercised at the same time and be back in time for your chicken pie," Jonah suggested quietly.

Kate mulled over the idea. She wanted to say no, she didn't need any help, but that would be petty and mean after Jonah had been so kind to her. Eventually she relented, telling herself that she would give Jonah and the rest of the outside world a wide birth after today. It didn't do to get reliant on other people's company, and she was perfectly capable of doing her own work, all by herself.

"Ok, thanks."

They rode, side by side along the beachside track, and Kate was beginning to feel a heat that she knew was not from the bright Cornish sun shining down on them. Spending near enough all morning with Jonah, plus the previous two weeks of having him sporadically pop over to help out, and now seeing him ride Pumpkin, she was starting to see him in a whole new light. His black hair was always out of place, and she noticed he was forever flicking it out of his eyes, and she felt herself blush when she wondered what it would be like to run her own hands through it. He was taller than her, which she thought was always a good thing, and he had a lean figure and sported a golden, sun-kissed tan. It was dawning on her that Jodie might have been right, and in the words of her sister, he was proper fit!

Then embarrassment flooded through her. He was so close to her, what if he could read her mind? She quickly directed Philippa onto the beach, announcing that it was time to turn home. She picked up the pace quickly; she needed the excuse of a short, sharp blast across the sand to justify her flushed cheeks. Jonah and Pumpkin kept up with her fast pace, and she was grateful to see that he was slightly breathless and his face flushed by the end of it.

That's it, Kate thought sternly to herself. *Absolutely no more daydreaming about Jonah. He's only here for another month or so, until the harvest is finished, so there's absolutely no point encouraging this...this...oh for heaven's sake...this crush!*

"I was thinking," said Jonah, interrupting Kate from her private thoughts. "If you're free next Saturday evening maybe we could go riding again?"

You're busy. Tell him you're busy. Did you not just tell yourself you were keeping your distance? Well, tell him that.

"Ok," she said out loud. "After I've finished work of course."

He replied with a warm smile and a twinkle in his eyes.

Theo

Theo, with his guidebook in hand, blended effortlessly into the crowd as he went about his own business exploring the ancient city of Pompeii. The week before, he'd been encouraged by James to visit the acropolis in Greece, and to his great delight, found a new passion for the classical world.

He meandered through the ruins, picturing what it might have been like thousands of years ago when the city was a busy, vibrant Roman settlement. He cast his eyes over to the impressive, imposing Mount Vesuvius, sleeping peacefully under the intense Italian sun, just nine kilometres away. He struggled to imagine the dormant volcano shaking the earth violently before exploding with molten lava, obliterating the neighbouring town of Herculaneum. And he shuddered involuntarily at the horror the Pompeiians faced the following day when the entire city was engulfed under the pyroclastic flow which burned its victims' lungs before death swiftly followed.

Theo was lost in the world of the ancient Roman empire for hours, until finally, he gave way to his hunger. After purchasing two books from the giftshop to further his interest and delve deeper into the classical world, he hopped on the tourist bus back to Naples.

Theo found a quiet café near the port where the cruise ship was docked and settled himself at one of the tables outside. He ordered a pizza margherita, stretched his legs out, and soaked up the beautiful costal view. He liked Italy. The food, the culture, the history - he loved it all. At the back of his mind, he hoped that one day, he could come back and enjoy it all again, with Jodie.

A phone call from his mother last month had buoyed his sinking spirit when she'd told him all about the wonderful evening she and his father had spent with Kate and Jodie. They all missed him, and Jodie had told her directly that she couldn't wait for his return. She was also pleased to report that Jodie wore the beautiful turquoise necklace he gave her for her birthday, then in a hushed tone, she admitted that she thought their plan might be working. Maybe the distance was making Jodie's heart grow fonder for him. She was also bursting with news regarding the new man, Jonah, and what a help he'd been to his father whilst he was away, easing some of his guilt for leaving his father in the lurch over the harvest.

After that phone call, Theo had made his mind up to confess his feelings to Jodie when he got home, and then whatever happened after that, at least he'd know. Once he'd committed to the decision, he felt his mind settle, his emotions steady and he finally began to enjoy his Mediterranean working cruise and appreciate his mini adventures exploring the different ports where the ship docked.

It was late when he finally climbed aboard the ship. The air was warm, the stars were twinkling brightly in the night sky, and with Theo not due to work until tomorrow evening, he decided to head to the outdoor bar area designated for staff. Soft music played and there was a low hum amongst his fellow staff as they relaxed and chatted in the open air. He saw Lynsey, and with an ice-cold beer in his hand, he made his way over to join her.

He liked Lynsey. She was funny and kind, always up for a laugh with him and James, and on top of her sultry, alto voice, she was a very clever girl. She was off to university at the end of the summer to study law. It seemed her life was mapped out for her, just like his. Her father was a partner in a top London law firm and her life goal was to work for him – it was what she'd always wanted. As much as she was enjoying the freedom of her six-month trip, she couldn't wait for her life to really begin once she returned home.

They chatted long into the night, and one by one, the other staff members took their leave until it was only the two of them left. Theo didn't notice to begin with; he was too immersed in the captivating conversation.

But then Lynsey slowly leaned forward, looked up at him under her dark lashes and whispered, "You can kiss me if you like?"

Theo was lost in the moment. The five cold beers he'd consumed were circulating through his veins and his heartbeat quickened when he realised her intentions. She looked beautiful under the soft glow of the moonlight, and he reached out his hand and tenderly traced his finger down the bare skin of her arm. On feeling his touch, she moved closer to him, closing the gap so that she was only inches away from him. He knew she was waiting for him to tilt his head, only slightly, for his lips to reach hers.

He snapped back like a lightning bolt had struck him. *What am I doing? What the hell am I thinking?*

"I'm sorry Lynsey, I have to go," he stuttered.

She looked crestfallen but said nothing as he hastily stood up and retreated to the safety of his cabin without looking back. Alone in his cabin, he pulled out his phone and saw a message from Jodie. He clipped open and a video pinged up of her old pony Cupcake nuzzling a young calf, with the message, *So Cute!* attached.

He scrolled through his photos to find the picture of Jodie and Pumpkin, and there she was, his beautiful, adorable Jodie. She might not be his girlfriend, but he knew she was the only girl for him. It would have been unfair of him to kiss Lynsey and lead her on. Not only would he never see her again after their cruise ship stint was up, but he felt nothing for her. She was a nice enough girl, and he might have had a momentary lapse in judgement because of the beer, but she was one hundred percent not worth risking any potential chance, albeit a slim one, that he might have with Jodie. And he certainly didn't want to have to tell Jodie about some girl he'd kissed whilst he was away. In his mind that would be a betrayal and something he would never do to her, and he hoped that whilst he was away, she was not kissing anyone else at home.

He looked at the calendar on his phone. Five weeks to go. Thirty-five days until he would be back in Cornwall, living next door to Jodie again. He propped his phone up on his bedside cabinet, picked up his guitar, pressed record, and sang Ed Sheeran's *Perfect* to Jodie, because to him, she was perfect. He found Jodie's number in his phone, attached the recording, and clicked send.

His head was pounding from the beer, his mind was racing from upsetting Lynsey, and his heart was longing to hold Jodie in his arms. Tossing and turning in his bed, his addled mind finally allowed him to fall into a fitful sleep.

He woke early the next morning bleary eyed and with a thumping head, and slowly, very slowly, his fuzzy brain pieced together the events of the night before. He grabbed his phone, but even with the time difference, it was still early, and Jodie had not yet seen his message. He felt relief flood through him, but his finger paused over 'delete message.' *Should I delete it? Would it be better for her to know that I'm missing her?*

He decided that impulsiveness was not his forte, especially with a thumping hangover, and so he figured he had about an hour before Jodie would be up and see his message. He would go and have some breakfast, take some painkillers, and hope that his muddled brain would engage in sensible thought before his hour was up.

He saw James and Lynsey in the breakfast room. No point ignoring the awkward situation. He still had to work with her for another month, after all. So he loaded up his plate then joined them at their table, just like he would usually do.

James slapped him on the back. "Good lord, you look just as bad as she does!" He pointed to a very grey looking Lynsey nursing her cup of tea. "Good night, was it?"

"Here," said Lynsey, throwing a packet of paracetamol at him. "If you're feeling anything like I am, you're going to need these." Then joining in with James's laughter, she continued, "Bloody great night, wasn't it Theo?"

Theo didn't know if she couldn't remember what happened, or if she was choosing to ignore the whole awkward situation, but either way, he was grateful. He laughed with them both, and along with Lynsey, filled James in on their evening, which he had to admit had been fun, until the end. But neither he nor Lynsey mentioned anything about the near kiss again.

Theo felt sorry for Lynsey. She was due at the kids club that afternoon, and with the way his own head was still throbbing, he knew he couldn't face a gaggle of over excited shrieking kids. Lynsey took her leave, announcing that she needed a few more hours kip before work, and with James off on a tour with some of the guests, Theo made his way outside. The Mediterranean sun was beating down, even at this early hour, but the salty sea breeze was cool, and he stretched out his aching limbs on a chair in the shade. A thought struck him that maybe Lynsey was even more embarrassed than him. It was, after all, her who had initiated the kiss. He may not have handled the situation well, and although his memory was bleary, he knew that it was her who made the first move. That in itself made him feel marginally better about the whole thing.

And now what to do about his voice message to Jodie? His eyes scanned the horizon. The bright sunshine was glittering down on the ocean. He closed his eyes and listened to the gentle waves lap against the side of the ship and it reminded him of being at Seal Cove. The refreshing sea breeze, the lull of the ocean, and the peacefulness of it all. After all of his travels over the past five months, Theo thought that there was nowhere as wonderful, or as special as his and Jodie's Seal Cove.

His phone bleeped in his pocket. Jodie's name pinged up on his screen. *Here we go.* He opened the message.

Loved it. Thanks Theo. Can't wait for you to sing to me properly when you get home. Only five more weeks to go! X

Relief flooded through him. She liked it! And with the thought of Jodie looking forward to seeing him again soon, he closed his eyes and drifted off into a much needed peaceful, deep sleep.

Jonah

Jonah was driving Mr Stevens' tractor up and down the field baling hay. It was a monotonous job, but after a while he fell into the rhythm of the tractor and allowed his mind to wander. The harvest was finally slowing down. He and Mr Stevens had been working every hour god sent over the previous week to get his grass fields mowed, turned and baled. A combine harvester had been hired for the wheat fields, and both Jonah and Mr Stevens had worked late into the night collecting the grain and safely storing it in Mr Stevens barn, it was to be his cattle's winter feed.

Jonah had wondered how Kate would manage her own harvest. His own workload was keeping him up until late into the night, then after just a few hours' sleep, he and Mr Stevens were back at it. You had to make hay whilst the sun shines! But Mr Stevens had assured him that Kate knew what she was doing. She only had fifty acres of hay to make, and she'd been helping her dad with the harvest since she was a small girl. He assured Jonah that she would manage just fine on her own. One morning, he and Mr Stevens were in the top field, with a glorious view for miles around, including a bird's eye view into Kate's farm, and Mr Stevens pointed out the little red tractor bumbling along, up and down the field.

"See," said Mr Stevens. "I told you she knew what she was doing!"

It had been a week since he last saw her, when he rode Pumpkin across the beach, and although they had planned to go riding yesterday evening, the harvest had taken precedence. Kate was the one who reached out to him first, sending him a message stating that Sunday would be better for her. She wanted to spend Saturday getting the bales of hay out of the fields and into the safety of her barn just in case the rain arrived earlier than predicted. Although disappointed, he couldn't complain; he was flat out with work himself. But the fact that she'd suggested to rearrange for the following evening gave him a spring in his step for the rest of the day.

Jonah placed the last large, square bale of hay on top of the great stack in the barn with the tractor loader. He lowered the pallet forks, turned the ignition of the tractor off and let out a deep sigh of satisfaction. He had done it. Every single bale of Mr Stevens' hay was now safe and secure, ready to be used to feed his animals over the winter.

He checked his watch. It was just under an hour until he was due to meet Kate at her farm. His exhausted body was aching, but his mind was buzzing with anticipation for his ride with Kate, and the surprise he had for her. He hurried inside, dropping his clothes as he went, then blasted his tired limbs with hot water from his shower. He watched the filth, dust, and grime swirl down the plug hole, and with it, the pressure and stress of his long hard slog of a week. Tonight was his night off, and work was now the furthest thing from his mind.

Showered, clean-shaven, and wearing fresh, clean clothes, he tacked up Jonty and filled his saddle bag with supplies. His time with Kate had finally arrived and he and Jonty clip-clopped along the country lane filled with anticipation. Jonty had been turned out in the paddock all week with Jonah's workload leaving him with no time to ride. But now, Jonah was relishing being back in the saddle of his trusted friend. The sight of Artie still in his paddock when he turned into Kate's farm caused his heart to sink into his boots. Had she changed her mind? Tying jonty up to the fence, he strolled over and knocked on the farmhouse door.

It swung open and Jodie beamed up at him. "Come in, come in," she said, ushering him over the doorstep. "She's running a bit late. One of the calves got its head stuck in a wire fence, silly thing. All sorted now though. She's in the shower. Cup of tea whilst you wait?"

Jonah relaxed instantly on hearing Jodie's explanation. "Yes, tea would be great, thanks."

He settled himself at the kitchen table whilst Jodie bustled about around him. *There's something different about her*, he thought. Without trying to stare, he darted his eyes over her every time he felt he wouldn't be noticed. Her hair's the same.

She's just as chatty and bubbly as usual. And then he spotted it, as if a great big banner was held across her belly. Good lord, she's pregnant! He was sure of it. Now he came to think of it, she no longer wore her tight-fitting jodhpurs and shirts that she'd worn regularly when he first met her. *And she doesn't ride her horse, and Kate flipped out when she tried to help him with the chicken coop. So, Kate knows about it.*

She was wearing loose fitted jeans with a very loose floral shirt, albeit pretty and in her usual style, just massive! He watched her pad about her kitchen, and every so often, the shirt pulled tightly over her stomach. She was definitely pregnant.

Kate broke through his thoughts when she came bounding down the stairs, apologising for being late, and Jonah got a delicious waft of her raspberry scented shampoo as she breezed past him.

"I'll just tack up Artie. Where do you fancy going?" she asked him.

Jonah knew exactly where he wanted to go. The question was whether Kate would agree.

"I was thinking the woods," he said tentatively.

"Blimey," replied Kate in surprise. "That's quite a hack. Do you think we'll get there and back before dark?"

"Well, I was thinking, if you wanted to, we could camp."

Jodie squealed in excitement. "Oh, what a brilliant idea Jonah! Dad used to take us camping there when we were little."

Jonah watched Jodie look at her sister, then at him, then back at her sister. "Kate," she continued, "should I pack you guys a picnic?"

"Actually, I have everything we need, if Kate wants to go?" He watched Kate mull over the idea of spending a night away from her beloved farm, and pregnant sister, in order to spend a night camping in the woods with him. He waited. He would not push her. This had to be her decision.

"Ok," she said simply, and Jonah nodded his acknowledgement.

They rode up Kate's track, across her field, and down the steep path to the beach. They had chatted initially about nothing in particular, but now they were silent, and Jonah was lost in his own thoughts as they plodded along the beach track with Flo skipping alongside them. The warm sun was beginning to set, and it looked like the huge ocean was swallowing it up. Instead of turning at the three-quarter mile point on to the beach, they continued along the track for another mile until it brought them on to country lanes.

Jonah was trying to push the thought far from his mind that his time working on the Stevens' farm was almost up. Theo would be home in four weeks, and then he would be out of a job and back on the open road, just him and Jonty. And as much as his wandering soul looked forward to his next adventure, he couldn't help thinking that Kate would not be with him. His feelings for her were growing stronger each time he saw her, and as the days ticked by, he found himself thinking of her and coming up with excuses to pop over to her farm. This was unchartered territory for him, and he felt at odds with his naturally solitary disposition.

The winding country lane finally brought them to the turning for the woods. A huge, three-hundred-acre woodland filled with wide open tracks for a good canter, leading to narrow overgrown paths for those who wished to explore off the beaten track. And it was down one of those paths that Jonah and Jonty had come across a large clearing, right in the middle of an overgrown, dense section of woodland which Jonah had chosen for the night's campsite.

They cantered fast along the tracks, unwinding from their hectic day to day lives, and when Jonah led Kate down the overgrown path, assuring her that if was safe for the horses, she let out a gasp of surprise when the isolated, private, clearing woodland appeared before them. The last rays of sunshine filtered through the leaves casting a warm, almost fairy tale glow, and with the gentle rustle of the leaves, the soft thud of the horses' hooves, and the tranquillity of the woodland, Jonah felt like they'd stepped into an enchanted forest. *I hope Kate feels that way too,* he thought.

They secured their horses, then gave them their hay net to munch. Jonah pulled a tarpaulin out of his saddle bag and strung it up between the branches to create a makeshift shelter, whilst Kate busied herself collecting sticks for a fire. Between them, in no time at all, their home for the night was ready, and the flames from the fire were giving them some much needed light in the dusky dense woodland.

"Sandwiches or cake to start?" Jonah asked Kate. Mrs Stevens had kindly whipped up some cheese salad sandwiches and given him two slices of Victoria sponge cake when he told her that he and Kate were going for an evening ride.

She smiled up at him. "Sandwich please, then cake for pudding!"

They settled down together on his tartan blanket, in front of the fire, and munched on their supper. *She's hard to read*, thought Jonah. She gave absolutely nothing away regarding her feelings, and he hoped in time that he would learn to understand this intriguing woman. The flames from the fire, just like Mrs Stevens' candle flames, brought out the fiery redness of her hair and Jonah couldn't help himself. He reached out and gently brushed her cheek with his fingers as he moved a wayward lock of hair out of her eyes and tucked it behind her ear. She didn't move. He kept his eyes on her, until she slowly turned and faced him, the flames dancing in her green eyes. He raised his hand again, and this time, placed his finger under her chin, tilting it towards him. He could feel his heart hammering inside his chest and saw a flush of colour reach her cheeks. She was so close to him, he only had to lean forward an inch, and his lips were gently brushing over hers. She responded, tentatively pressing her own lips against his. And then she pulled away. Jonah felt her shiver from the cold, and carefully placed a blanket around her, leaving his arm resting around her waist. Slowly, in her own time, she leant towards him and rested her head on his shoulder. Never, in the whole of his life, had Jonah felt so intoxicated, so utterly bewitched by a woman. And he began to wonder if his reason for being back in England, his unexplainable driving force to be in Cornwall, was not just about his beloved Jonty, but because of Kate.

He heard her breathing steady, and after gently moving her hair out of face, he saw her eyes were closed and she was fast asleep. It gave him encouragement that she trusted him enough and felt comfortable enough in his company to let her guard down and fall asleep against him. He reached out, and praying that he wouldn't disturb her, grabbed a log from the pile and dropped it onto the fire. With the sound of the horses munching, the fire crackling, Flo snoring softly and Kate sleeping in his arms he closed his eyes, content that he was exactly where he should be at exactly the right time.

Jodie

Jodie was lying amongst the golden straw in Pumpkin's stable, and with her hand resting protectively on her belly, she contentedly watched her horse munching hay. She felt her baby kick, a feeling she never tired of, and a feeling she wanted to savour, knowing full well that it would not last forever. In three and a half months' time she was going to be a mother.

"And Theo will be a father," she said out loud to her trusted confidant.

Guilt swept through her over her deliberate choice to keep the baby a secret from Theo. She'd been so sure at the time that she was doing the right thing. That her discretion had enabled Theo to enjoy his six months away. She was sure he would never have gone if he'd known, and that deep down he would have resented her for curtailing his fun and freedom by tying him down at such a young age. As soon as she'd seen a second line appear on the pregnancy test, she knew that having a baby was exactly what she wanted. It was what she'd always wanted. She'd waited for the wave of fear, shock, and maybe anxiety to engulf her, but it didn't. She couldn't wait to be a mum and it didn't bother her in the slightest that she was so young. But Theo was different. His future had been mapped out for him, right from the beginning. And she knew that taking on his family farm was no small feat. He would have a huge amount of responsibility on his shoulders, and although it was what he wanted, over the next few years he would have a lot to learn in order to run his business as successfully as his father did. A baby was most definitely not on his mind. And the responsibility of both her and the baby, on top of his farm might be more than Theo could cope with.

But then he sent that message. She'd heard the emotion in his voice. She instantly knew he was homesick, no matter how upbeat and chirpy his messages were. He was her best friend, and had been since forever. She knew him almost as well as his own mother did. And he could not hide his longing for home, and his farm, and she secretly prayed, for her also.

"I'm starting to think I made the wrong decision, Pumpkin," she confessed to her mare. "Maybe it was unfair of me to make the decision for him."

She continued to gently stroke her swollen belly and thought that maybe Theo would want to place his hand on her stomach and feel their baby kicking, just like she did. But she'd taken that choice away from him. Her mind swirled with her constant over-analysing of the whole situation. Round and round went her thoughts, to the point where she felt like whichever decision she made, it would not have been the right one.

Maybe she didn't know Theo quite as well as she thought she did. Maybe he was just like her? Maybe he was content with his lot in life? And maybe, once the initial shock wore off, maybe he'd actually be pleased with her news?

Or maybe, she thought, with nausea rising within her, maybe he's met someone new and exotically beautiful on the cruise ship? Maybe he doesn't want to return home at all? A brand-new exciting life might be waiting for him somewhere else... and with someone else.

She struggled to her feet and closed the gap between her and Pumpkin. Wrapping her arms around her, and burying her face in her mane, she squeezed her horse tightly. Hearing his beautiful voice singing her favourite song, just for her, had sent her hormones flying in every direction. And with it had come even more confusion.

"Who knows what will happen," she whispered to her horse.

The sound of hooves clip-clopping down her drive pulled her away from the heartfelt conversation she was having with her horse, and with a downward glance at her ever-growing belly, she decided to remain hidden in the stable. She knew the horse's footsteps did not belong to Kate and Artie. Kate, along with her ever loyal Flo, had taken the Land Rover and trailer to collect a potential new horse for training, and then she'd promised to swing by into town to pick up groceries and feed supplies on her way home. Jodie was steadily feeling more and more guilty with the continuous work load her sister was having to complete on her own due to her pregnancy, and the secrecy of it. She was adamant that she would not tell Theo whilst he was away, and Kate supported her decision, even though it meant her list of jobs piled high on her already overflowing plate. So, for now, hiding her condition meant that until Theo returned home, and the cat was finally let out of the bag, she would remain at the farm.

"Kate, Jodie, anyone home?" Jodie heard a familiar voice call out.

"Hi Jonah, I'm in with Pumpkin," she replied.

She didn't want to be rude. Jonah had been so kind to her, helping to fix her hen house, and what a wonderful job he'd done. He'd even collected eight hens for her the day after its completion. Every morning she enjoyed looking out of her kitchen window to watch her hens roam freely in the garden, and she immensely enjoyed baking with their lovely, fresh golden eggs. She leant against the stable door, all signs of her pregnancy hidden, and as she heard his footsteps heading towards her, she hoped she would not have to move.

"Jodie, hi. I've been sent by Mrs Stevens to personally deliver this," he said, handing over an envelope with both hers and Kate's name written in Mrs Stevens' familiar handwriting. Before she had chance to reply, or even question what the mysterious envelope contained, Jonah continued, "Is Kate here?" She watched his eyes scan the empty yard.

Keen not to drag the conversation out any longer than needed, she forced herself to squash her curiosity regarding the hand delivered note – she would find out soon enough anyway - and decided to reply only to his question of Kate.

"She's gone to view a horse. The owner's having a few issues with it and asked if she'd take it on for a few weeks training," she replied. She thought she saw a flicker of disappointment glaze across his eyes, but it was so quick, she couldn't quite be sure. And in that moment, she wondered why Jonah had not been invited to go with Kate, he was great with horses... And then more guilt flooded through her veins. *Well, maybe if I wasn't so caught up in my own self-absorbed world, a place that I have selfishly dragged Kate right into the centre of, I'd know the answer to that question.*

"Ok," he replied simply. Then seeming to realise she had no more information to offer him with regards to Kate, he continued, "I'd best be off; Jonty and I are on our way to check the sheep up on the moorland. See you again soon." And with a brief exchange of smiles, he was gone.

Jodie turned her attention back to Pumpkin, and whilst she ran her hands over her golden fur, inhaling her sweet horsey scent, she wondered why Kate seemed to be giving Jonah the cold shoulder after their camping trip two weeks ago. Jodie thought Jonah's idea so wonderfully romantic; she'd almost been a little envious of her sister, watching her ride off into the sunset with the handsome cowboy. But she was pleased for her sister. Kate deserved a break from the farm, and she most certainly deserved the attention of a kind man, who as far as Jodie could tell, was absolutely smitten with her.

"So, what's burst the bubble of happiness for her?" she asked Pumpkin. And she resolved to find out as soon as Kate returned. She wished that she could have Artie and Pumpkin tacked up, ready and waiting for when Kate got home. It was a gesture which always signalled that one of the sisters needed to talk, and without question, the other would climb into the saddle, and wait. They would ride side by side in companionable silence until the time came for secrets to be shared and problems discussed.

Jodie sighed a deep, heavy sigh. The one and only thing she missed whilst being pregnant was being able to ride. She missed their idle plods. She enjoyed soaking up the far-reaching countryside views, and the rhythmical sound of Pumpkin's iron-shod hooves clip-clopping around the country lanes. She couldn't wait for an early morning gallop across the broad stretching beach, and to watch the seals play under the rising sun from Seal Cove cliff top, on horseback.

"It won't be forever," she promised her horse, as she opened the stable door.

Pumpkin walked quietly beside her until they reached the paddock gate where Artie, little Cupcake and the orphan heifer calf were waiting expectantly for her.

Leaning against the paddock gate Jodie retrieved the letter from her pocket.

Dear Kate and Jodie,

It was so lovely to see you both for our little dinner party all those weeks ago. Where has the time gone! Mr Stevens and I are sorry that we haven't seen you since. We have all been so busy with work and the harvest. Jonah has kept us up to date with the success of your own harvest and we are so pleased that he has been able to rebuild your chicken coop and help with other odd jobs around the farm. Jobs I know that Theo would have gladly helped you both with if he had been here.

Mr Stevens and I are very excited about Theo's return in just two weeks' time! We've been told not to collect him from the ferry port, or to fuss! He'll be catching a coach from the port and Mr Stevens will pick him up from town at seven. He's been away for six months, of course I'm going to fuss! We would love for you both to join us for a little welcome home party for him. A few of his school friends, along with their parents, will also be coming along. The plan is for everyone to arrive at six and be ready and waiting for when Theo arrives at seven! Please say that you will both come?

I look forward to seeing you both soon,

With love

Mrs Stevens xxx

Jodie read the letter again. She felt like a sharp pin had just burst her safe, private little bubble. The bubble she had cocooned herself in, with the help of Kate and within the sanctuary of her farm, since Theo left. Reality was now firmly hitting home. In just two weeks' time she was going to have to face up to her decision of keeping the baby a secret from Theo, and his lovely mum and dad, and in the pit of her stomach, she felt an ugly feeling form with the thought that none of them would be very happy with her. Feeling rather glum, she cast one last look over the contently grazing horses, then slowly headed into the house. She had cakes to bake and dinner to make. She and Kate would need plenty of sustenance to get through the long talk they would inevitably be having tonight with regards to Theo's party. And then of course she was keen to get to the bottom of the whole Kate and Jonah situation.

Kate

Bumbling along in her battered old Land Rover, Kate was grateful for the distraction of Xander. A local woman had seen him and fallen in love with him on the spot, and Kate could see why -he truly was a stunner of a horse. Xander was a 16.1 hand, bright bay, thoroughbred gelding, straight off the track. And presently, he was far too much for his new owner to handle. She was having problems with him bolting off at flat-out gallop as soon as they hit any sort of track or open space, and his breaks were currently non-existent. Kate knew he was doing just what he had been trained to do. Run. And to run as fast as his legs could carry him.

But he wasn't a racehorse anymore, he was now an adored pet, and he must learn the ropes for his new job, as a lady's riding horse. Secretly, Kate couldn't wait to get her hands on him. She could feel excitement building in her for what was to come. Driving home, with Xander in the trailer behind her, she pictured the wide, open space of the beach calling her. Once she had sorted Xander's breaks out, the thought of galloping a racehorse flat out across that beach brought butterflies to her stomach and a thrill flushing through her veins.

It was the first time she had truly felt excited since losing her father. Her overwhelming grief had not been fully processed due to Jodie's bombshell pregnancy. And she had carried it with her, privately, ever since. Not only did she have the responsibility of the farm and her sister, plus her little niece or nephew that would be joining them all very soon, she had the added pressure of Jonah. Her heart skipped a beat on thinking about him. She'd never felt the flurry of emotions for any other man before like she'd heard other girls describe. She'd had a couple of boyfriends over the years, but they never came to anything. She was too set in her ways and too committed to her business. Until Jonah came along. There was something about him that made her feel indescribably drawn to him, and she had a natural desire to be in his company. It was something she had never felt before, and she was beginning to realise what those girls had been on about. Their camping trip in the woods only increased her already burgeoning feelings for him, and for a brief moment, after she felt his lips gently brush her own, she'd imagined what it might be like for him to be her boyfriend. For her to have someone to support her and help her and Jodie manage their farm and run their business. And also someone, dare she even think it, to have fun with. But it had been a fleeting daydream. Jonah was a natural wanderer; he'd told her that himself. And he would only be working next door until Theo returned. That had always been the plan.

Then there was the small matter of Jodie getting bigger and bigger by the day. She couldn't allow Jonah to keep popping over to the farm anymore or Jodie's secret would be out. Nor could she confide in him; the risk of Jonah saying anything to Mr and Mrs Stevens was too high. So she'd made the hard decision to push Jonah out of her mind and put to rest any silly ideas she held of potentially dating him. It was for the best. Between work, horses, and Jodie, she didn't have any spare time to offer him anyway. It was best to keep her distance until he left, which was only a few weeks away anyway. Making excuses over the previous week not to see him had been a real slog for her. And in some ways, she'd felt mean because deep down she desperately wanted to see him, and to ride with him again. But she couldn't let herself get attached to him, knowing that he would be moving on to another farm again soon. It would expose her to heartbreak, and she'd had enough of that to last her a lifetime as it was.

The phone call about Xander two days ago had perked her up immensely, and now that she'd met him, and was taking him home, she saw a little light twinkle at the end of her seemingly relentless dark tunnel.

After safely unloading and securing Xander in a paddock, with Flo standing quietly by her side, she watched him buck and squeal and zoom about his new abode. Grinning at the prospect of training him, she left the rambunctious horse to investigate his paddock and headed into the house to tell Jodie all about her day.

The kitchen table was laden with delicious treats, and on seeing them all, her positive mood began fade away. There was always something delicious waiting for her at every mealtime, but excessive baking always meant that Jodie was stressed in some way, and she silently prayed that it wasn't anything to do with the baby.

"Jodie, we're home," she called out, helping herself to a chocolate brownie as Flo settled herself in her bed.

Jodie padded down the stairs, her wet hair tied up in a towel on her head, and her cheeks still pink from her shower. Kate knew she had something to tell her by the way she was anxiously shifting from foot to foot.

"Is something wrong with the baby?" Kate blurted out.

"Oh no!" Jodie replied. "No, it's not that at all. We had a visit from Jonah today, he gave me this," she said, hurriedly handing over a letter.

Kate felt herself relax. If the baby was ok, she could face anything. Taking her time, she read the letter from Mrs Stevens, word for word, whilst Jodie hovered nervously beside her. She felt herself blanch when she read that Jonah had kept them up to date about their harvest.

Has he now? she thought crossly. *And what else has been keeping them up to date with?* Is that why he was so keen to come and help Jodie? Had Mr and Mrs Stevens sent him round to spy on them?

She was furious. Not only did she feel insulted that Mr and Mrs Stevens, and lord knows who else, might think her unable to manage her own farm and business, but her own pride took a bashing, feeling foolish about Jonah. She genuinely liked him, but now she questioned if he'd only sought out her company because the Stevenses had asked him. Maybe it was just out of pity? She shuddered with shame.

"Kate," whispered Jodie. "Are you ok?"

Kate swiftly pulled herself together. She couldn't put any of her upset and frustration on Jodie. Jodie needed comfort and support during her pregnancy. She turned to her sister and smiled.

"Of course." Then she broached the actual reason why they'd received the letter. "So what are we going to do about Theo's party?"

"Cake, and a cup of tea first," announced her sister. "Then we'll make a plan."

Kate woke early the next morning. She peeked through her sister's open door to see her sleeping soundly. She and Flo crept down the stairs, stopped briefly in the kitchen to grab a slice of Jodie's lemon cake for breakfast, then silently slipped outside into the chilly autumn air. It was still dark, but Artie heard her coming, and she found him waiting patiently for her at his gateway.

"Good morning, beautiful boy. Let's go riding!"

Alone, with only her horse and dog for company, Kate watched the sun rise through the misty air from Seal Cove cliff top. As the weak light filtered through the murky morning sky, she spotted two seals resting on their private sandy shore. She breathed the fresh air deeply, and, pleased with her seal sightings, she asked Artie to follow the track down to the beach.

Kate and Jodie had talked long into the night and formed their plan. Waking up this morning, she was relieved to feel that she still stood by their decision. She knew her gut instinct would kick in, first thing in the morning, and if she'd made the wrong decision, she'd know. But this morning, surrounded by the restful sound of her horses' hoofbeats and the gentle lapping of the waves on the beach, with her loyal dog skipping alongside her, she felt at ease.

The girls had spoken to Mrs Stevens' over the phone last night. They thanked her for the invitation, told her they thought a surprise party was a wonderful idea, and of course, they would both love to come. Part one of their plan was complete. It was the truth; they did both want to go. Part two, however, would involve fibbing, but they both agreed it couldn't be helped. On the day of the party, only Kate would go, giving the excuse that Jodie was dreadfully poorly. They would say that Jodie couldn't wait to see Theo as soon as she was well enough. They thought that her fake illness could last a couple of days without Theo and his family getting suspicious about Jodie not being first in the queue to welcome Theo home in open arms, which is what everybody would be expecting. It would at least buy them a little extra time, allowing Theo to settle back into his work routine on the farm before he learned of what the future now held for him. Jodie had also tentatively tried to bring up Jonah, but Kate was so exhausted of thinking about the whole situation herself, she didn't have the energy to go through it all again with her sister, especially after the party plan was sorted. Her sister pushed, knowing that something wasn't right between them, but truth be told, there wasn't much to discuss anyway. He was leaving, so that was that.

Kate directed Artie off the track and down onto the sandy beach. She wasn't in the mood for galloping; she was enjoying the gentleness of her surroundings. She, Artie, and Flo, slowly plodded along the beach as if they had all the time in the world. And for the first time since she could remember, she did. She wasn't in a hurry and her daily routine for the cattle and horses would be waiting for her, no matter what time she returned. She relaxed into her saddle, cast her eyes far out to sea, let go, and cried. Hot tears streamed down her burning cheeks as she finally allowed herself to think about her father, and the enormous gap he'd left in her life. He was her father, her business partner, and her best friend, all rolled into one. They had just clicked and been so content in each other's company. They held the same values and views on nearly everything to do with their business, and if they ever differed in opinion, they quietly accepted to agree to disagree. Kate knew that her father was irreplaceable, and she would now have to spend the rest of her life without him. Her broken heart ached. It ached with grief, and it ached with the insurmountable love she held for him. And she cried for the grandchild that he would never get to see, or love. She knew he would have been just as much of a doting grandfather as he had been a father, and Jodie's baby would never get to enjoy him. The utter unfairness of it all.

Artie carried her steadily up the track and back to Seal Cove point. Kate took one last glance towards the mesmerising ocean view; the place where she had scattered both of her parent's ashes. And then she turned Artie towards her farm. She stopped at the gateway marked 'private,' and she soaked in the view before her. The fields, the stables, all of the animals, and the house. Her inheritance and her family farm. Her entire world was held in that small pocket of beautiful Cornish countryside, and she loved all of it. Every single blade of grass, each and every animal that called her farm their home, and her cosy little farmhouse.

"I'll look after it, Dad," she whispered out loud. "The farm, our animals and Jodie. I'll look after all of them. I can promise you that."

Kate, Artie, and Flo made their way across the fields, down the track and back on to the yard. There was work to be done.

Theo

Theo felt anticipation build within him as the coach turned down the familiar road towards his local town's bus station. During the two-hour journey from Plymouth dock yard, he'd reminisced about his time away. Six long months. It had been hard, he'd admitted that to himself, but in equal measure, it had also been the adventure of a lifetime. The bustling cruise ship, filled to the brim with every kind of holiday maker imaginable and the wonderful Mediterranean ports he'd explored were a far cry from his family farm, nestled in the Cornish countryside. His trip had certainly opened his eyes to what the world had to offer, and what adventures could be had. He'd visited Greece, Italy, France, and Spain. He'd even taken a day trip with James to Morocco. They'd caught the ferry from Spain when they were given a day off, and what an experience that bustling North African market town was. Every single one of his senses came alive amongst the exotic spices, vibrant colours, and the bustling chaos of the city. They'd even ridden a camel! He recalled how three camels were lined up, not far from the Moroccan ferry port of Tangier, ready and waiting for the tourists to arrive. He and James had laughed hysterically when they climbed aboard the camel sitting down, then the unfamiliar rocking motion started as the camel heaved itself, and them, up on its feet. He certainly had some happy memories to take home with him. But it also reaffirmed that home was where he truly wanted to be. He now knew without doubt that he wanted to take over his family farm, and he couldn't wait to get started.

He couldn't wait to tell Jodie about his travels. Especially Italy, and how much he adored it. The food, the culture, the history, he loved it all. And he hoped that one day they would go there together. He wanted to share the enjoyment and all the wonderful experiences that Italy had to offer with her. Fingering the pretty bracelet he'd bought for Jodie from a little market stall in Naples, he thought of her. She'd been at the forefront of his mind every day since he left. His mother was right, distance most certainly did make the heart grow fonder. He only hoped that the same would be true for Jodie, and that she was as equally excited about his return. He closed his eyes and a picturesque Italian cobbled street appeared in his mind's eye. He pictured Jodie and imagined her sitting opposite him at one of the traditional boutique outdoor tables. They were sharing a delicious pizza and the warm Mediterranean sun sparkled on Jodie's golden ringlets.

He sat up eagerly when the coach driver announced his stop, his eyes scanning the pavement next to the bus stop, half expecting Jodie to be waiting for him. And he felt the disappointment like a kick in the gut when he only saw his dad, smiling and waving at him as soon as the bus turned into the road.

His dad pulled him straight into his arms as soon as he stepped off the coach.

"Theo! My boy! Welcome home."

Theo returned his father's embrace. "Hello, Dad!"

Swinging Theo's rucksack over his shoulder, his dad gestured for him to follow him to the car. "Now, I know you told us not to make a fuss, but I thought I'd better warn you…"

"Mum's made a fuss!" said Theo, laughing along with his father as he finished his sentence.

"Yep, you guessed it. She's invited a few friends over to celebrate your return. I hope you don't mind," his dad said with a concerned look in his eyes. "She just couldn't help herself! She's so excited about you coming home!"

Theo had an inkling that something like this would happen. He knew his mother well, and he adored her for it. And at the back of his mind he thought that Jodie would have been the first person on his mum's guest list for the party. She would be waiting at the house for him!

His mum flung the front door open before he'd even stepped out of the car, and within moments she'd swept him up into her arms. He breathed in her familiar, homely smell, and relaxed into her arms. He'd missed her. She gripped his arms then pushed him away from her, holding him at arm's length.

"Look how tanned you are!" she exclaimed. "And so handsome!"

He blushed under her open praise as she ruffled his hair, then ushered him into the house.

Theo was warmly welcomed by his family and friends as soon as he stepped into the house. They shook his hand, slapped him on the back and hugged him closely on greeting him. But as he scanned the room, and met each smiling face, he could not see Jodie. His heart plummeted into his boots. He had been so sure that she would be there. So sure that she would have been the first one, pushing everyone else out of the way, to wrap her arms around him and welcome him home. He'd imagined it so vividly in his mind that he could feel the weight of her small frame in his arms, and almost smell her intoxicating jasmine and honey scent from the shampoo she always used. He noticed Kate weaving her way through the crowd, making her way towards him, and on making eye contact, she smiled broadly and opened her arms. He returned her gesture and embraced her tightly, just as he might a big sister. That is what their relationship had always been like, and being an only child, he was grateful for it.

"Jodie is so sorry she couldn't be here," gushed Kate. "She's so very desperate to see you and totally devastated that she can't be here tonight, but she is just feeling so rotten. She's got a terrible cold and not only is she exhausted with it, she didn't think it fair for her to come to your mum and dad's house and spread her germs around! As soon as she's up and about, she'll be straight over to see you."

Theo was crushed with disappointment and worry. What if she can't bear to see me after what happened? What if I've ruined any chance I might have had with her? Or is she genuinely ill and did want to be here?

His mind swarmed with questions that only Jodie could answer, and he also wondered if Kate knew what had happened between them. Jodie told Kate everything. Surely she would have told her? But if Jodie was upset, why was Kate being so nice to him? If he'd upset Jodie, and Kate got wind of it, there's no way she would let it lie. She'd tell him in no uncertain words exactly what she thought of him. But here she was, squeezing him tightly in her big sisterly way. Women really were a mystery to him.

Theo did not have long to dwell on his thoughts. An unfamiliar figure approached him, with his hand held out, keen to introduce himself.

"Theo. I'm Jonah. Your mum and dad have told me so much about you. It's great to finally meet you."

"Mum and Dad have told me a lot about you," replied Theo, shaking his hand, grateful for the distraction, and even more grateful that Jonah immediately launched into safe conversational territory; the harvest and the farm.

It was nearing midnight by the time the evening began to wind down and everyone took their leave, and Theo was exhausted from his busy day; he couldn't quite believe it started on the cruise ship! And now here he was, climbing up the stairs to his own bed.

His mum greeted him eagerly when he wandered into the kitchen, bleary-eyed, at seven o'clock the next morning.

"Theo, darling, what can I make for you for breakfast? Anything at all, you just name it!"

"Anything?" replied Theo grinning, keen to make the most of his mum's generosity on his first morning back.

"Pancakes?" asked his mum.

She knew him so well! "Yes, please, Mum!"

Whilst tucking into his delicious pancakes, dripping in sugar and lemon, Jonah strolled into the kitchen for his morning cup of coffee.

"Your dad's gone into town to pick a part up for the tractor," announced Jonah. "Do you fancy riding up to the moors with me to check the sheep?"

Theo couldn't wait to get started, nor could he wait to get back into the saddle. Six months without being near a horse now seemed like a very long time.

"Definitely," he replied.

Jonah nodded in response, and after swigging down the last dregs of his coffee, "I'll go and tack the horses up, see you in five," and he was gone.

Relaxing into Marty's saddle, Theo patted his father's horse gently on the neck as they climbed the steep track towards the moors. He reflected that it was about time he got his own horse. He'd outgrown his childhood pony, Patch, a couple of years ago, and with the plan always being that he would work away for six months, he'd borrowed Marty, or his mum's horse, Gem, in the meantime. But now he was home for good, it was time to find his own. Plus, it would give him a good excuse to go and visit Jodie and Kate; if anyone knew of a good horse for sale it would be them. And then he could find out for himself if Jodie really was as keen to see him as her sister said she was.

Theo voiced his thoughts; it was his subtle way of bringing Jodie into the conversation. His mum had told him that Jonah had fixed Jodie's chicken coop, and although he was pleased the job had been done, he was slightly envious that it was Jonah who'd done it and not him. He was keen to hear anything that Jonah might have to say about Jodie. Conveniently, Jonah seemed happy enough to discuss horses, and Theo was pleased to hear how highly he thought of Pumpkin after riding him out with Kate. He also praised Jodie's baking with gusto, and Theo was very much looking forward to sampling any new creations she'd come up with during his time away.

Once reaching the moors, the two men worked in companionable silence, checking, and counting the sheep, assuring themselves that they were all present and correct. It wasn't until they were making their way home that Jonah mentioned Kate. Just as subtly as he himself had mentioned Jodie. Theo's curiosity was piqued at the thought that something might be going on between them. His loyalty firmly lay with Kate, but he was obliging enough to share his opinions on her excellent horse training skills and how she'd always looked out for Jodie.

Thinking that maybe Jonah was also keen to find an excuse to go over and see the sisters, and as far as women were concerned, there was always strength in numbers, he offered, "Maybe we should pop over to see the girls tomorrow? I can take Jodie the bracelet I bought her in Italy, and some flowers to cheer her up if she's still feeling poorly, then we can talk to Kate about finding me a horse. What do you think?"

He waited patiently for Jonah to mull over his offer, his mind spinning with the prospect of what might happen if he turned up unannounced on Jodie's doorstep. But he couldn't wait any longer. He had to know how she really felt after what happened on the cliff top all those months ago.

"Yes, ok. Your dad's been kind enough to find me some work on a farm about ten miles away. I start next week. It would be nice to say goodbye to the girls," replied Jonah.

The men nodded to each other in agreement. Theo felt his stomach tie itself in knots. Like it or not, tomorrow he would find out exactly what Jodie thought of him, and he was hoping and praying that even if they would never be anything more than friends, that she would still, at least want that. He couldn't bare it if she no longer wanted his friendship. Tomorrow would most definitely be judgement day.

Jonah

Jonah was grooming Jonty down after his hard ride that morning over the moors to check the sheep. With three missing, Jonah and Jonty had worked hard to cover the undulating ground in order to find them, then herd them back to the rest of the flock. As he meticulously brushed his horse, his mind repeatedly went over when and how it seemed to have all gone wrong with Kate.

One minute they were sitting in front of a campfire with him holding her in his arms, and the next, she was giving him the cold shoulder. She rebuffed every suggestion he made for them to spend time together, be it working on her farm, riding, training horses, or just sitting on the cliff top enjoying the view. She'd turned him down each and every time, and for the life of him, he couldn't fathom why. He liked her. He liked everything about her. Her tenaciousness, her practical business mind, her work ethic, her exceptional skills with horses, and of course, she was beautiful. He thought he'd made his feelings perfectly clear on their camping trip. And he thought she knew him well enough to understand that he did not go sharing his thoughts and feelings with just anyone. And he admitted to himself that he was hurt by her actions. He was leaving in less than a week. Mr Stevens had been so kind when he went to him with regards to finding another job. He could have gone anywhere. He could have tacked up his horse, and with his trusty backpack strapped to his back, idled down the farm lane, and gone, in any direction he chose, and just seen where he ended up, like he usually did. But no, he'd specifically asked Mr Stevens if he knew of any work going in Cornwall, so he could be close to Kate. And as foolish as he now felt, he didn't want to leave her without clearing the air. Theo suggesting they go together gave him the confidence boost he needed. Having Theo at his side would make the situation a whole lot easier. He would be polite, say his goodbyes, and if it was truly what Kate wanted, he wouldn't bother her again. Seeing her one last time would at least give him some closure.

His mind was also spinning with curiosity over Theo and Jodie. He liked Theo. From the short amount of time he'd spent with him, he'd worked out quickly why he was so well liked within the local community. He was both kind and hardworking, but not exactly subtle. His feelings for Jodie bored out of him like a bright red beacon! And Jodie's interest in Theo had not been lost on him either. Thinking back, every time he'd been in her company, one way or another, she'd found a way to bring him into conversation. And then there was her pregnancy which no one other than Kate seemed to know about. He'd deliberately pushed the whole matter from his mind. He knew for sure that Kate would not appreciate any kind of intrusion into hers and Jodie's private lives so bringing the topic up with her was completely out of the question. And then her distancing herself so blatantly from him meant he couldn't have asked her anything anyway, even if he wanted too. And so, he'd quelled any ideas of unravelling the pregnancy mystery, it wasn't his business anyway. But now, his mind buzzed with curiosity. Why would it be such a secret? And then it was like someone had flicked a switch.

"Oh my word, Theo's the father!" he said out loud to Jonty. It was all so clear to him now. The girls had been keeping their distance from the Stevenses, who were supposedly great family friends who loved and adored the girls. Mrs Stevens often told him about the antics Jodie and Theo used to get up to when they were little, and how she was constantly over at their farm. Kate was often there too, learning all she could from Mr Stevens when she was younger, and lending a helping hand whenever she was needed.

Jonah went over and over it all in his mind. For whatever reason, Theo obviously didn't know about the baby. And the girls couldn't risk Mr and Mrs Stevens finding out then reporting back to him. But why didn't Theo know? That was one question he definitely couldn't answer.

Feeling that his loyalty lay firmly with the girls, Jonah checked his watch, then swiftly tacked up his horse again. "Sorry boy, I can't let you rest just yet." Theo was busy helping his dad and would be for another hour or so. They were due to meet for lunch in the farmhouse kitchen before they rode over to see the girls. If he left now, he'd have plenty of time to get to the sisters beforehand and warn them of Theo's impending visit.

The farmyard was empty on his arrival, but in the quiet air, he heard Flo scratching from the inside of the front door, alerting the household of his arrival. Flo was never far from Kate's side, and no doubt the sisters were nestled in their cosy kitchen having their mid-morning break. He inhaled deeply to try and steady his nerves. His confidence in his impulsive decision was beginning to wane now that he was about to face the girls. And he fervently hoped that he'd pieced all the pieces of the Jodie jigsaw together correctly, otherwise he was going to look very foolish indeed.

Kate opened the door within seconds of him knocking, her brow furrowed in both confusion and annoyance. But even so, he couldn't help his mind involuntarily flitting back to holding her when the flames of the crackling fire illuminated her golden red hair as she rested her head on his shoulder. And he could not shake the yearning of wanting to hold her close to him again.

"Hello Jonah," she said, making no attempt to move away from her half-opened door and let him in. "What can I do for you?"

"Actually," he said. "I'm here to see Jodie."

"I told everyone at the party, she's poorly," she replied curtly. "You can't see her. I'll pass on any message for her though."

He took a breath. *Here we go...* "Theo will be popping over to see Jodie later on today. He wants to bring her flowers, and a present he bought her in Italy, as a surprise to cheer her up. I thought it best to come and warn her, what with her being pregnant with Theo's baby and everything."

Kate stood opened mouthed before him; her green eyes boring into him on hearing his statement. But before she had a chance to reply, Jodie came up behind her and placed a hand on her sister's shoulder.

"It's ok," she said softly to her sister, then turned to face him. "Jonah, you'd better come in."

Once the initial awkwardness had passed, and Jodie finished busying herself about the kitchen getting everyone tea and slices of cake, she finally sat down. She first looked to her sister, who'd remained silent since opening the door to him. He noted the brief nod she gave Jodie, and after being given her sister's signal of approval, the whole story came tumbling out.

Jonah sat quietly and let her talk, and as her story unfolded, all he could think of was how sensible, how level-headed, how mature the little seventeen-year-old in front of him was. He'd been a complete wreck at seventeen, and he would certainly not have been capable enough nor responsible enough to bring another life into this world. But Jodie, she was something else. And her baby, well, it was going to be a very lucky baby indeed having Jodie for a mum.

"Thank you for coming to warn me of Theo's plans," said Jodie, placing her warm hand over his. "It really was decent of you. And now I must tell Theo everything. I'll message him now and ask him to come over."

Within moments of her sending the message, her phone bleeped with Theo's reply.

"He'll be over in half an hour," she informed them all. Then she looked up at him with her big, innocent blue eyes and asked, "Will you stay until he gets here?"

"Of course," he replied. He was rewarded with her warm smile, then she announced that she looked a mess and that she must go and get changed.

Rather selfishly, Jonah was grateful that she left, leaving him and Kate alone in the kitchen, and he could finally get to the point for the reason of his visit.

"Have you told Mr and Mrs Stevens about Jodie?" Kate asked frostily. "We know you've been telling them things about us."

Jonah was rather taken aback with her icy tone, not to mention affronted that she'd pegged him down as a gossip. He'd never gossiped in any way, shape or form with her, so why on earth would she think he'd do it with anyone else?

"Of course not," he replied, and he couldn't help the defensive tone that accompanied his words. "I only pieced it all together this morning, and I came straight over here to tell Jodie."

"Maybe you didn't know about Theo, but you knew she was pregnant. Did you go straight back and tell them when you worked it out?" she continued, and Jonah felt that she was almost trying to provoke an argument with him.

He relaxed his frame, lent back in his chair, and spoke softly. "I've said nothing, Kate. I promise you. What happens over here on your farm is none of my business, nor anyone else's. I thought you knew me better than that."

But his gentle tone did nothing to deter Kate's accusatory glare. When Jodie returned to the kitchen, Kate immediately softened her posture and turned her attention to her sister, and before any more could be said, Flo jumped up and ran to the front door. All eyes peered out of the kitchen window; Theo and Marty were coming up the drive.

"I'd better go now, Jodie," Jonah said. "It's not fair on Theo for me to be here when he finds out."

And in her sensible, calm way, Jodie smoothed down the pretty top she'd changed into, then nodded in agreement.

He offered Kate a warm smile on his parting, but it was not returned, and so with a heavy heart, he let himself out of their home. He waved hello to Theo, briefly informed him that Jodie was inside waiting for him, and then he mounted his horse. His eyes scanned the yard, the stables, and the nearby fields, dotted with cattle and horses, all of which he'd come to love. A place that, up until it had all gone inexplicably wrong, he'd relished being in. Being here, with Kate and Jodie, was one of the few times he'd ever felt truly content. And he'd hoped that it would have been a place that he would have returned to, through all the changing seasons, as his relationship with Kate blossomed. But for whatever unfathomable reason, it seemed that his daydreams would not be coming to fruition.

He and Jonty slowly plodded down the drive, enveloped in a cloud of sadness over Kate. He felt the loss of what could have been weigh heavily on him. He forced himself to acknowledge that the excitement and anticipation he'd begun to feel and enjoy when seeing her and thinking about her was now over. The world around him was quiet, apart from Jonty's iron-shod hooves crunching over the autumn leaves scattered on the country lanes, and he wallowed in his melancholy mood all the way back to the Steven's farm. He groomed his hardworking, loyal horse down, then turned Jonty out in his paddock, finally giving him the much-needed rest he'd promised him after his busy day. Watching Jonty skip and buck and play in his paddock, he suddenly realised that he didn't even say goodbye.

Jodie

Hearing a loud knock on the front door, Jodie remained seated, using the kitchen table to safely hide her bump. She watched Kate slowly stand, and then wait for her to signal that she was ready. She looked her sister straight in the eyes and nodded. It was time to see Theo.

Her heart skipped a beat when Theo came bounding into the kitchen, his excitement on seeing her positively oozing out of him. And how handsome he looked. His skin was the colour of golden honey from all those months in the sunshine, and Jodie felt herself blush when she became the full focus of his attention as soon as he saw her. She had been the epitome of calm before he arrived. Sharing her story with Jonah had helped prepare her for this moment, and in some ways, she was grateful that it had finally arrived. Her obsessive thoughts going round and round in her mind could finally call it quits. But now, seeing him standing right in front of her, she felt a shyness come over her that she'd never felt in his company before. Six months was a long time to be apart from someone, but not only that, Theo had come home looking like some sort of golden Greek god, whereas she was now the size of a small whale, and getting bigger still. She felt self-conscious as he eagerly smiled at her, and her well prepared speech momentarily left her, so all she could do was stare right back at him.

Kate must have sensed her floundering. She took control of the situation for her by accepting his flowers and gift on her behalf, then ushering Theo to sit down opposite Jodie. Then she babbled away with whatever small talk seemed to pop into her head whilst she made a pot of tea and placed the sandwiches Jodie had made earlier on the table.

She couldn't stand the forced jollity of her sister, or the awkwardness, any longer. She pushed her chair back, stood up and blurted out, "I'm pregnant, Theo."

An eerie silence followed as Theo's eyes gazed down to her swollen stomach, then flicked up to meet her own, before falling back on her belly again. Kate moved behind her, protectively placing her arm around her. But she needed to deal with this on her own. She couldn't hide behind her big sister forever.

"It's ok, Kate," she said, gently patting her sister's arm. "I think Theo and I need to talk about this on our own now." Her sister gave her one last squeeze, then silently slipped out of the kitchen.

She looked imploringly at Theo, willing him to say something, anything, but he just stood there, staring at her.

Theo's crisp voice eventually broke the silence between them. "All this time. Six months, Jodie! And you never said a word. We messaged each other almost daily; how could you keep this from me?"

"I didn't want to ruin your trip," she replied.

"Ruin my trip? For the love of god, Jodie, you're having a baby. My baby. Didn't you think I had a right to know? Didn't you think that I'd want to be here and support you? Do you honestly think I'd have given a damn about the trip if I'd known what was going on back home."

When he put it to her like that, with such passion, such conviction in his voice, her excuse now seemed rather pathetic. But his speech was not yet over.

"I trusted you, Jodie. I've always trusted you above anyone else. I can't believe you've lied to me like this. Does anyone else know? My parents?" he asked, with questioning eyes.

She quietly explained to him that only Kate knew. And Jonah. But Jonah had worked it out for himself; all she'd done is confirm his suspicions when he came over to the farm this morning. And then she did her best to assure him that her intention had always been for him to be the first one to know, apart from Kate of course, as soon as he returned home.

"I need to go now, Jodie. I've got a lot to think about." She watched him turn on his heel and leave.

She sat back down, rested her head in her hands and allowed her tears to flow. She knew she didn't have the right to expect anything from him after what she'd done. But deep down, she admitted to herself that she had been secretly hoping that he would wrap his arms around her and tell her that he loved her, and that everything was going to be alright. But in between her heavy sobs, she felt her sisters' arms snake their way around her shoulders, and it was Kate who told her that she loved her, and Kate who told her that everything was going to be alright.

Once her emotional outburst was over, she listened to Kate's comforting words, and acknowledged that she was probably right. Theo needed time to get over the shock. She'd had six months to come to terms with having a baby, but Theo had only just found out. And once he'd had time to process her news, she was sure everything would work itself it. They were talking about Theo after all. Lovely, kind, Theo. Her best friend. And it was then that she wondered if he would still want to be her best friend after what she'd done. And had her deliberate betrayal ruined her chance of anything more with him? She slowly unwrapped his gift that Kate had left on the kitchen counter. Holding the delicate silver and turquoise bracelet in her hand, tears swelled in her eyes at how thoughtful and how truly lovely Theo really was.

Jodie slept fitfully that night, tossing and turning in her bed, worrying herself silly about what the future might hold with Theo. Hearing her sister's early morning alarm go off, she pushed back her bed covers; it was time to get up. The sisters met bleary-eyed in the kitchen, and as they pottered about together making tea and toast, Kate asked, "What are you going to do about today?"

She'd completely forgotten. With everything that had been going on over the last week, the secrecy and fibbing for the party, Jonah's unexpected arrival, and then telling Theo, her six-month scan had totally slipped her mind.

"I think you should tell Theo. Give him the option to go with you if he wants too. I can still take you if you need me to though. It's up to you," said Kate.

Feeling guilty enough as it was, there was no way she was going to keep the scan from Theo as well. She quickly checked the calendar hanging behind the kitchen door.

"It's not until mid-day, I'll message him now. Then he'll have plenty of time to decide what he wants to do."

Jodie baked all morning and checked her phone at least two hundred times. She'd sent Theo's message at six o'clock in the morning. Kate came in at nine thirty for her mid-morning cup of coffee, and to hear of any update. But Jodie had nothing to share. They agreed that Kate would check back in at eleven, the time they would need leave in order to get to her appointment on time. And then finally, just after ten, her phone bleeped.

I'll pick you up at eleven.

She stared down at the message desperately trying to decipher if he was still cross with her. Did he genuinely want to come with her, or was he just doing what he thought to be the right thing? Had he forgiven her yet? But the perfunctory message gave nothing away.

He arrived, right on time, but he wasn't his usual self. He was reserved, formally polite, and they remained quiet in the car apart from him informing her that he'd told his parents. The silence continued between them during the twenty minutes wait in the hospital waiting room, and he just quietly followed her when the sonographer called her name and led them into a private hospital room. Jodie settled herself on the bed, making small talk with the friendly sonographer, trying to hide the current animosity between her and Theo.

"Ok then, Mum and Dad, are we ready to see baby?" said the sonographer, as she squeezed the cold jelly on to her stomach.

And then there was her baby, as clear as anything, pictured on the screen in front of her. The sonographer turned up the volume so they could both hear the thumping noise of its healthy heartbeat. With her eyes fixed on the screen, she felt Theo's hand slip into her own.

"Oh Jodie," he whispered. "Our baby."

"And would you like to know the sex?" asked the sonographer.

"Oh yes," replied Jodie, and at exactly at the same time ,Theo said, "No."

The sonographer smiled at them both, "so what's it going to be?"

Jodie hadn't even thought to ask Theo his feelings on finding out the sex. She and Kate had discussed it repeatedly, ever since her first scan, and Kate whole heartedly agreed with her decision of wanting to know. But Theo didn't. As much as she was bursting with anticipation to find out, after everything she'd done, she could at least give him this.

"On second thoughts, I think we'll wait," she said firmly.

Daring to look at Theo, she glanced towards him to meet his eyes, and she was rewarded with a smile. It was the first smile he'd given her since he'd come home. And Jodie felt herself glow on the inside from receiving it.

On leaving the hospital, Theo reverted back to the reserved, quiet version of himself, which unsettled her. Determined to break through the barricade he'd put up between then, she broke the silence between them.

"Shall we go for a walk when we get home?"

"Ok," he replied simply, and then the silence resumed for the rest of the car journey.

She led the way, with him quietly following her, along her farm track, across the fields and through the gate marked private at the top of the cliff path. Then she carefully weaved her way through the gorse bushes and down the hidden track to their secret spot above Seal Cove. The place where it had all begun. Jodie thought that for them to push through their current predicament, they had to start at the beginning. They had to talk about what happened the last time they were here in order to move forward.

They sat, side by side, just like they always did, and watched the seals bob up and down in the water below.

"I'm sorry, Jodie," Theo eventually said.

Surprised, she turned to him and said, "Whatever for! You've done nothing wrong. It's me who needs to do the apologising."

And then to her astonishment, Theo explained to her exactly his reasons for being the one at fault. How he'd taken advantage of her when she was vulnerable after losing her dad. He should never have overstepped the mark like he had. And he certainly should never have left without talking to her properly, about everything that had happened between them before he vanished into thin air for six months. For leaving her confused about how he felt for her. So confused that she felt she couldn't tell him about the baby. He should have been honest about his feelings for her before he left. He should never have gone.

Jodie felt overwhelmed with all the hurt and guilt Theo had been carrying with him for such a long time. Not once had she ever felt taken advantage of, and she assured him that what happened was because both of them wanted it to happen. And as far as she was concerned, she couldn't wait to have their baby.

Jodie felt relief flood through her that finally, after all these months, they were being honest with each other, and sharing their feelings. As they sat in companionable silence, looking out across the beautiful ocean view, Theo placed his arm around her and pulled her in close to him. Resting her head on his shoulder, she closed her eyes, and for the first time since losing her father, she felt her spinning mind settle. A calmness descended, and she felt at peace.

Kate

Kate was standing on her yard, absolutely fuming, as she watched Xander's owner drive away. She'd been so excited that morning to show off how well he was doing with his training, so well in fact, that she would not hesitate to call him the perfect gentleman. He'd been with her for two months now, and although they'd had a few ups and downs along the way, he was proving to be a very well-behaved horse. She'd invited his owner over to ride him and see his remarkable improvement for herself. It had been unfortunate timing, a car backfiring on the nearby country lane just as his owner had given him the correct aid to transition up to canter in the makeshift paddock school. And he'd spooked. Not bolted off with her like she tried to imply, but a simple spook that any other well-behaved regular riding horse might have done. A couple of quick strides and a little skip to the side, nothing that any run of the mill rider couldn't cope with. Blimey, she'd even jumped herself on hearing the loud bang penetrate the quietness of the countryside. But the owner wasn't having any of it. Clearly, she couldn't forget his initial behaviour when he came to her straight off the track. And now she'd just gone and driven off, leaving her to deal with Xander. She was not very happy about it at all.

She clomped her way across the yard and into the house, muttering her frustrations as she went. She found Theo sitting at her kitchen table, reading the instructions on how to put together the baby's crib.

"Everything ok?" he asked, instantly picking up on her grumpy mood. Kate was grateful to have someone to vent her anger and frustration too, and she quite happily launched into her views on poor horsemanship and her low opinions of Xander's owner. "And she was barely on him ten minutes so now I've got to exercise him myself, as well as Pumpkin!" *I bet he wished he hadn't asked,* she thought ruefully, after her rant finally came to an end.

"I could ride him?" he offered. "You ride Pumpkin, we can go together if you like?"

Jodie's taking a nap, she won't mind me popping out for an hour."

Half an hour later, she and Theo were galloping across the moors like a pair of crazy people. Poor old Pumpkin was struggling to keep up with Xander's quick acceleration and racehorse speed, but that didn't stop Kate from enjoying every minute of it. Theo slowed Xander down so they could eventually catch up and give Pumpkin chance to catch her breath.

"He's a cracking horse!" exclaimed Theo. "What are you going to do with him?"

"I'll have to sell him. The owner has kindly dumped him on me until I can find a buyer. As soon as possible, apparently, so she can then use the money to buy the next love of her life," scoffed Kate.

"I'll buy him," announced Theo.

"What. Really?" she asked, not believing her luck.

Theo explained about how he'd been looking for a horse since he came home but was yet to find one suitable. But having now ridden Xander, well, he definitely thought he was the one for him. Plus, Xander and Pumpkin seemed to get along rather well, and it would be Jodie and Pumpkin who he'd be riding out with as soon as Jodie could get back in the saddle.

Well, well, well, thought Kate. Maybe the day wasn't turning out so bad after all!

"Brilliant," she said. "I'll let the old bag know as soon as we get back. Consider him yours!"

Kate and Theo chatted away as they rode alongside each other heading for home, and Kate agreed wholeheartedly with Theo's idea of taking Jodie away for the night. He'd found a spa, not too far away, that offered relaxing massages for pregnant ladies, plus the use of their heated swimming pool. He thought it would be nice for Jodie to get away and enjoy a bit of pampering before the baby arrived. Buzzed up from her exhilarating ride, plus Theo taking Xander off her hands, she encouraged him to call the spa as soon as they got home and find out if they had a room available tonight, then a full day of pampering for Jodie could commence tomorrow.

Kate couldn't help but get swept up in Jodie's excitement about her treat night away with Theo. She helped her pack her bag, reassured her that she and Flo would be fine on their own for the night, then she stood on her doorstep and waved them off. She thought back to how far Jodie and Theo had come in six weeks. What a nightmare the first few days had been. Not only had she consoled a heartbroken Jodie whilst Theo came to terms with everything, but she'd had to take charge of the situation with regards to Jodie facing Mr and Mrs Stevens, once Theo had explained the whole situation to them. But luckily, the thought of a little grandchild soon to be tottering around quickly smoothed over Jodie's decision of neglecting to mention her pregnancy for six months. And now Mrs Stevens was in full swing helping her and Jodie in any way she could, including knitting booties and baby outfits with any spare time she had.

As she closed the door behind her, she leant back against it and smiled. A whole night to herself!

"Come along Flo," she called out, as she skipped up the stairs, a long hot soak in the bath was now the first thing on her agenda.

She borrowed some of Jodie's bath salts and candles, climbed into the steaming water, closed her eyes, and relaxed. She was so very pleased for her sister. There had been months and months of stress and confusion over when and how to tell Theo, and they'd had countless conversations about Jodie's concerns about Theo's involvement. Would he want to be involved? If so, how much? Would he still want to be friends with her? Would he want more than friends? And up until Theo came home, and voiced his opinions himself, neither she nor Jodie could possibly know the answer, but that hadn't stopped them over-analysing every possible outcome. How pleased she felt that all was now well, and they could prepare for their baby's arrival together.

With Theo now sharing the load of hospital appointments and preparations for the baby, not to mention taking excellent care of Jodie, Kate found herself with more time for her mind to wander about the direction her own life was going. *Too much time*, she mused. She'd been so wrapped up in Jodie, she'd not given her own life any thought for months. Seeing Theo and Jodie working together towards their own future seemed to enhance her own sense of being alone.

She stretched out in her bubble bath, closed her eyes, and thought of Jonah. And what a bitch she'd been to him. She couldn't deny it, no matter how much she wanted too. She'd behaved horribly towards him. He'd been nothing but polite and helpful to both her and Jodie, never asking for anything in return for all the jobs he did for them on the farm. Not to mention how kind and thoughtful he was whenever he was alone with her, and romantic. What a wonderful evening she'd had camping with him. No one had ever made her feel as special as he'd done on that night. And how had she repaid him? She ignored him, gave him the cold shoulder, and accused him of spreading gossip about her and Jodie. She felt herself flush with shame by her own actions. And not that it was in any way an excuse, but she knew she'd used him as her scape goat.

She'd been so frustrated, and angry, and full of grief for her father. Not to mention both physically and emotionally exhausted with everything that was going on with Jodie. All those pent-up emotions had inexplicably come out as malice and unkindness towards the one person who was actually supporting her through it all. She could see that now. Jonah was quiet and unobtrusive, but he was there, always at the right time, and always when she needed him. She'd well and truly taken advantage of his good nature.

She felt her eyes prickle with tears over the fact that she hadn't even had the good grace to say goodbye to him. Theo let slip two weeks ago that he was working on a farm only ten miles away. She couldn't believe it when she heard. She'd fabricated such a web of hurtful thoughts towards him about spreading rumours and him leaving her after the harvest that she'd never bothered to ask where he was going. Ten miles! That was close enough for them to meet on horseback. They could have seen each other all the time, and slowly built a relationship together. But it was all too late now. Her pride wouldn't allow her to ask Theo which farmer he was working for. She was too embarrassed to ever face him again. She held her breath and sunk deep down into her bath, willing the hot, soapy water to wash her mortification and shame away.

Flo's short sharp yip brought her away from wallowing in her melancholy.

"What is it, girl?" she asked her dog.

Flo barked loudly, then bounded towards the closed bathroom door signalling that she wanted to be let out. Then she barked again, this time more aggressively, and continued to bound between the bath and the door.

Kate heaved herself up and out of the bath, concerned with how her dog was behaving.

"Ok Flo, I'm coming," she said softly to the dog, trying to reassure her. As soon as she opened the bathroom door, Flo raced out, flew down the stairs, and began barking again at the front door. Kate felt a chill fall over her. Something wasn't right. She quickly threw on a pair of jeans and sweatshirt then hurried down the stairs to see what had got Flo all worked up.

She saw it as soon as she flung her front door open. Smoke was bellowing out of her barn, and flames were lapping the opposite end from the stables, the area where her winter hay was stored. But the way the wind was blowing, and the fierceness of the flames, she knew it wouldn't be long before it spread through the entire barn.

"Oh, holy hell," she shrieked. "The horses."

She didn't even wait to put her boots on. She sprinted across the yard, slowing only to fling open the gate of the closest paddock, and with Flo at her side, she ran into her barn, undoing each stable door bolt as she went.

The horses were skittish and panicked from the thick smoke descending on them and the roar of the ever-nearing fire. They bolted instantly, scattering haphazardly around her yard, dancing and prancing, their eyes wild with fear. She called to Flo, her ever loyal dog, who switched to work mode instantly. Between them, they guided the flighty horses through the open gate and into the safety of the paddock. She pulled out her mobile phone, ready to ring the fire brigade, just as she was doing a head count of the galloping horses.

"Oh dear god, Cupcake and the calf," she shouted out in disbelief.

All thoughts of her phone call forgotten, she scanned the yard for her beloved childhood pony and calf. And then she heard it, a throaty nicker coming from inside the barn.

"They've got into the bloody winter hay," she said out loud to her dog.

She turned to see the flames eating their way through her barn. "Stay," she commanded her dog. There was no way she was risking Flo following her back inside. On seeing Flo sit instantly by the paddock gate, obeying her command, she pulled her sweatshirt up over her nose and mouth, then headed back into the burning barn.

Jonah

Jonah and Jonty were down in the valley doing the evening check of Mr Conrad's sheep. The setting sun glowed gently, with pinks and yellows illuminating patches of the dusky sky, signalling that the day was coming to an end. *Red sky at night, shepherd's delight,* he mused, enjoying the natural display of colours the world offered him that evening.

Mr and Mrs Conrad owned one hundred acres of steep valley fields, where they grazed their flock of seventy-five sheep. Plus, they had one hundred acres of fairly decent, flattish fields suitable for arable crops, and their fifty head of cattle. They also had a small piggery, Mrs Conrad's passion, where she bred pedigree saddleback pigs for both the show ring and the table. A mixed flock of ten chickens, three barn cats, and Mr Conrad's two working collie dogs made up the entirety of the Conrads' animals.

The Conrad's were getting on in their years. Although elderly, they were still sprightly for their age, but having a young man about the place was very much needed. And Jonah liked them very much. He worked hard, enjoying all the variety that their farm had to offer, and they treated him like one of the family.

Jonah turned Jonty to make their way back up the steep track to the farmyard after checking all sheep were present and correct, and as they slowly plodded home, his mind turned to Kate, like it always did, once the hustle and bustle of the day had calmed. He couldn't help himself. And no matter how many times he thought back and reminded himself of her aloofness and coldness towards him, she still brought out feelings within him that he'd never felt before, including the constant sadness, deep in the pit of his belly, that it had all turned out so wrong. He couldn't help it, he loved everything about her. Over the past six weeks, he'd come up with all manner of excuses to visit her, or maybe drop in and see Theo and the Stevenses with the possibility of accidentally bumping into her, but he knew that pushing someone like Kate was not the way to win her. And so, as the days ahead of him slowly ticked by, he hoped the enforced time apart would heal his aching heart.

"Jonah, love, supper will be ready in five minutes," called out Mrs Conrad, when she saw him and Jonty plodding through the farmyard, bringing his thoughts back into the present.

He smiled and nodded, then watched her scurry back into her kitchen to finish preparing their meal. He dismounted his horse, ran his hands over Jonty's warm neck in praise for his day's work, and then he felt it. A wave of foreboding washed over him, and his gut instinct kicked in like a lightning bolt. Something was wrong. Something was very wrong. Every fibre in his being was telling him to go to Kate. He swiftly untacked his horse and turned him out in his paddock, then without explanation, he opened the farmhouse door, and shouted out that he needed to borrow their car. It would take far too long to ride over to Kate's farm, even if he bypassed the roads and went cross country. Plus, his hardworking horse was tired after his day on the farm, and he would not ask him to carry him, flat out, over hedges and gates unnecessarily. As he expected, the keys were hanging in the ignition of the little blue car, and within moments, he was on his way. His unease of what he might find on arrival mounting with each mile he travelled.

The smoggy, smoke-filled air confirmed his premonition whilst he was still one mile away, and speeding up, he saw the mass of flames tearing through Kate's barn as soon as he turned into the driveway. Cupcake and the calf were loose, scampering around the yard with wild eyes, the other horses, he noted, were alert, but quiet, grazing at the far side of the paddock. Flo, was whimpering, rushing forwards and backwards towards the burning barn. Oh dear god, Kate's inside.

He took off his jumper, sploshed it into the nearest water bucket, and dripping wet, tied it as best he could around his nose and mouth, then sprinted into the barn, calling Kate's name as he went. The intensity of the heat was unyielding as he dodged the flames in search for Kate. The fire crackled and roared as it relentlessly devoured the wooden beams, leaving destruction in its wake.

He saw her bare foot poking out of the tack room doorway. Its stillness sent shivering chills of fear down his spine. In three strides, he was beside her. She did not respond to him repeatedly calling her name, and in one swift movement, he scooped her up in his arms just as he heard an almighty crash coming from the far end of the barn. The barn was crumbling under the fire's merciless consumption and Jonah, laden down with Kate, was not quick enough to move his arm when a burning beam came crashing down, searing his skin as it went. He smelt his own burning flesh before tightening his grip, holding her closely, and protecting her as best he could from the flames. His eyes stung from the smoke, and his breathing laboured through his now dry jumper as he pushed his way through the circling flames until finally, he felt clear air fill his lungs.

On auto pilot, he pulled out his phone and called the fire brigade, before his aching body collapsed against the paddock gateway, with Kate cradled in his arms.

Jonah stirred to the sound of women talking in hushed tones, filling his muddled brain with confusion as to where he was and why he was there. Slowly opening his eyes, he found himself faced with unfamiliar surroundings. Blinking under the glaring lights shining directly down on him from the ceiling, Jonah shuffled to evade their brightness.

"He's waking up," Jonah heard, before feeling a hand rest gently on his shoulder. "Jonah, love, can you hear me? It's Mrs Conrad. You're in hospital, love, but don't you worry about a thing."

Then he felt a warm, comforting hand slip into his own, "I'm here too, Jonah. It's me darling, Mrs Stevens. You'll be right as rain in no time, Mrs Conrad and I are going to look after you."

He felt a piercing pain in his arm, his head ached and then he felt a jolt zap right through his body as his befuddled mind started to awaken and the memories came flooding back. The fire. Kate. Oh dear god...Kate. His already thumping head throbbed relentlessly as his thoughts turned to Kate and he remembered the last time he saw her. He felt physically sick thinking back to holding her limp body against his chest, then nothing. His memory stopped and his mind went blank.

"Kate," he stuttered, attempting to lift himself up and push through the pain that shot through his arm.

"She's going to be fine, love," said Mrs Conrad, placing her hands on his shoulders to encourage him to lie back down.

"She's with the doctor now," chipped in Mrs Stevens. "I saw her before coming to see you. I promise you, she's fine. You need to focus on getting better yourself right now. You've got a nasty burn on your arm and the doctor said you're to stay here over night so they can keep an eye on you after all the smoke you inhaled."

Jonah relaxed back into his bed on hearing that Kate was alive, the fear of losing her ebbing away with each reassuring word and comforting touch from Mrs Stevens and Mrs Conrad. Both women, one after the other, leaned forward and placed a kiss on his forehead, before telling him to rest, but reassuring him that they would be back soon to check on him.

Jonah drifted in and out of sleep, his busy mind contemplating how he'd somehow ended up with two wonderful, motherly figures in his life. Both Mrs Stevens and Mrs Conrad had welcomed him into their homes and treated him like one of their own, right from the get-go. Yes, he'd worked hard for them on their family farms, but he was paid for that. Neither of them needed to care for him in the way they had, and looking back, Jonah couldn't quite believe how lucky he'd been, with them both. And now here they were, in his time of need, right by his side, fussing over him like any mother would. Not that he'd know of course. He'd lived a long life without one. But it was how he'd daydreamed it would be, and it felt nice. For once in his life, he didn't feel alone.

Those two women made him feel like he meant something to them, and he liked it. And he made up his mind, there and then, that if Mrs Conrad would allow it, he would continue to work and live at her farm for as long as she needed him. And he would be only a few miles away from Mrs Stevens, to be on hand if she ever needed him. For the first time in his life, Jonah felt that it was time to put down some roots. Then his thoughts turned to Kate. And his aching heart beat within his chest as he sleepily dreamed of holding her in his arms again, if she'd ever let him. He pictured her fiery red hair, and her piercing green eyes and vowed to himself that he would see her again. If he was to settle at Mrs Conrad's farm, and call it his home, which he so desperately wanted to do now, he needed closure with Kate. The farming community was a small one and he would no doubt bump into her at one of the local villages or livestock auctions, so parting on good terms could only be a good thing. And then, maybe, one day, they could be friends again. With thoughts of galloping across the beach with Kate, and wild picnicking on the open moorland with their horses together, Jonah finally drifted off into a deep, restful sleep.

Two days later, Jonah was sitting at Mrs Conrad's kitchen table tucking into a hearty full English breakfast, and thoroughly enjoying being fussed and pampered by Mrs Conrad. The topic of him staying was brought up by Mrs Conrad herself when he was still in hospital, and she informed him that she would be taking him home as soon as the doctor would allow it. He liked the way she just presumed that he would be going back to her home, and he felt a warm glow filter through him when he overheard her talking to the doctor. She'd tutted in annoyance when the doctor mentioned Jonah going back to work too soon, and she explained that yes, he worked on the farm, but he was like a son to them, and without doubt he'd be given the very best care at home with her and Mr Conrad.

Although no words had actually been spoken, both the Conrads and Jonah knew that he would be staying, permanently. Not having any children of their own, Mrs Conrad seemed to relish in having someone to adore and look after, and Jonah was happy to oblige. The situation was new to all of them but from the moment she brought him home from hospital, Jonah allowed Mrs Conrad to claim him as her own, just as he did her. He watched her expertly knead the bread, in preparation for their evening meal of homemade soup accompanied by crusty bread dripping in butter, and he felt contentment in every fibre of his being. All those months ago, when his intuition and gut instinct had guided him all the way to Cornwall, he'd found Jonty, his best friend, and he'd found Mr and Mrs Conrad, two people who seemingly wanted him unconditionally, and Kate. He'd not yet seen her, although Mrs Conrad assured him that she'd tried to see him before she left the hospital, but he was asleep. And that, in itself, gave him hope. She'd actively chosen to seek him out. Surely that could only be a good thing. He knew in that very moment, cosied up in Mrs Conrad's kitchen, yet again, he was exactly where he should be at exactly the right time in his life.

"Oooh, it looks like you've got a visitor love," said Mrs Conrad, peering out of her kitchen window, pulling him out of his thoughts and back into the present.

"Really, who is it?" He craned his neck, but was unsuccessful at seeing who it was through the tiny inch of window that Mrs Conrad wasn't blocking.

"It's Kate."

Theo

Theo, along with his father and Jodie, was standing in front of the fire ravaged barn, struggling to take in the catastrophic sight before him. He couldn't believe that the mass of burnt ash and rubble was once Jodie and Kate's immaculate, well-structured barn. He shook his head in disbelief and fury as he listened intently to what the Chief Fire Officer was telling them.

"Chinese lantern," stated the officer. "Bloody nightmare they are. Look at the damage," he said, with a sweeping arm gesture over the destroyed barn, "that one little flame can make."

"Yours wasn't the only barn to go up that night. Although we got to that one in time so minimal damage for that farming family," he continued gravely. "We try and inform people regularly about the dangers of the wretched things but so many people think that our concerns don't apply to them. It's a constant battle trying to educate people, but no matter how hard we try, some just don't listen, and this is the result."

Theo could hear the frustration in the officer's voice, and he could feel Jodie bristle beside him on hearing the news. This was by no means an accident, but the result of someone else's ignorance and stupidity. And he knew that they were all thinking the same as him. A fire of this colossal scale could have ended up with much more than a destroyed building. Lives could have been lost. More specifically, had it not been for Kate, the lives of all their horses, and had it not been for Jonah's bravery, Kate's life, too.

The thought of what could have been weighed heavily on him, and he subconsciously placed his arm around Jodie and protectively pulled her closer to him whilst they all offered their thanks and said goodbye to the fire officer.

Theo watched his father mount Marty, then waved goodbye. He wanted to make sure Jodie was ok before leaving her. Taking her by the hand, he led her into the house, gestured for her to sit down, then busied himself making them both a cup of tea.

"You feel guilty too, don't you," Jodie said.

He knew what she meant, but he didn't. If he hadn't taken Jodie away to the spa that evening, then she would have been here when the fire happened. He shuddered involuntarily at the thought of what might have happened to Jodie and their baby if she'd been caught up in the chaos of trying to save the horses. She would have done anything and everything in her power to save Pumpkin, that he was sure of. He felt guilty that he'd not been there to help Kate, of course he did. She was like a sister to him, and he would do anything for her. But his priorities now lay very firmly with Jodie, and deep down he was grateful that he'd taken her away and kept her safe from the devastating fire. However, he knew that Jodie would not think like he did.

"Yes," he replied simply. It wasn't a fib, not really, just not the whole truth.

"And about Jonah," he continued. "None of us really kept in contact with him after he left, apart from Mum."

"I know," said Jodie, with a sombre look on her face. "And I really liked him. He was so kind to me and Kate whilst you were away. I feel like I dropped him like a stone as soon as you got back! And that was very mean of me."

Theo rested his hand reassuringly on Jodie's arm. He felt exactly the same way. Jonah had helped his family during their time of need when he was off gallivanting around the Mediterranean. He'd worked hard, every single day, and he'd always found time to help his mum with any extra jobs she needed doing around the house, not to mention all the help he'd given Jodie and Kate. And despite the short amount of time he'd spent with him, he did genuinely like him. Then to top it off, whilst he and Jodie were off being pampered at the spa, Jonah had somehow, miraculously turned up and saved Kate. He'd gone into that burning building and hauled her to safety with no consideration for himself. If it wasn't for him, well, it didn't bear thinking about. He felt the outcome of the fire would have taken a very different turn indeed if Jonah hadn't showed up.

"I'm going to bake him a cake!" Jodie announced. "Then we can take it over to him tomorrow," she said, with determination in her voice. "We can't go today, Kate's gone over to speak to him, and I don't want to step on any one's toes. But I hope to God that the pair of them sort things out! I never really got to the bottom of why it all fizzled out between them, but as far as I'm concerned, they are perfect for each other!"

Theo smiled to himself at Jodie's suggestion, and how in Jodie's world, everything was fixed with a large slice of homemade cake! And he had to agree with her. Who wouldn't want a slice of one of her delicious creations.

"Great idea!" he replied enthusiastically.

Happy that Jodie was busy and content in her kitchen, he kissed her cheek, said his goodbyes, and headed off to work. Climbing into Xander's saddle, he set off across the farmland, and through the gate at Seal Cove cliff top, making his way up to the moorland to check his flock of sheep. He and Xander paused briefly to watch the seals play in the water beneath them, a view that he'd enjoyed since forever, and a view that he would soon witness with his own child at his side.

His impending fatherhood was always at the forefront of his mind. In all honesty, he couldn't quite believe his luck, and in some ways, he'd got everything he could ever wish for. His beloved Jodie loved him! And they were starting a family together. His wonderful mum, like always, supported him whole-heartedly, and somehow effortlessly smoothed things over with his initially furious father. He knew his father had only been thinking of the practicalities of it all. How young they both were, and the lack of financial stability between them both. Plus, the fact that Theo still had an awful lot to learn about running his business. The timing, he admitted to himself, and only himself, wasn't ideal. He worried constantly about his finances, and how he would be able to support Jodie and the baby. And then there was the matter of where they would all live. Ever since his return, and since he'd managed to get his head around Jodie's pregnancy, and all the secrecy, they'd been taking things slowly. He rarely stayed over at Jodie's house, and if he did, it was always in the spare room. Their commitment to each other was clear, but for the time being, Jodie's health throughout her pregnancy and the baby's health were their only concerns. The progression of their relationship could wait until after its arrival.

He desperately wanted them all to be together, and to live as a family, but where that would happen, he didn't know. He lived with his parents. Happily. He'd had no reason to consider moving anywhere else for the foreseeable future. He wondered whether Jodie would consider moving in with him and his parents? He knew his mother would be on hand to help with anything and everything Jodie and the baby might need. But Jodie was never far from Kate at any given moment, so he couldn't see her leaving her own family farm any time soon. Perhaps Jodie would consider Theo moving in with her and Kate? Or option three, he considered – could they ever afford their own home? But that led to even more questions that he was unable to answer at that moment. Even if he could afford it, where would it be? With horses and livestock, both of them needed to be on hand and close to both farms at any given moment. Round and round it all went in his mind, and with no one to share his thoughts with, his merry go round mind ceased to stop.

Everyone seemed to only focus on the baby's arrival. Not one person had mentioned what would come afterwards. And with the fire destroying Jodie and Kate's barn, everyone's main focus was on that, just as it should be, he told himself. Without a barn to stable the horses over the winter months, and their entire supply of winter hay gone, the girls were in a predicament that no farmer should ever have to face. Decisions need to be made, and soon.

He watched a lone seal dipping and diving in the clear water down in the cove. The weakened sun filtered through the murky autumnal clouds and for a brief moment, he felt calm. The fresh, chilly breeze circled him, and closing his eyes for a moment he listened to the choppy waves crashing against the rocky coastline. He'd enjoyed the special view through all seasons, year in, year out. It didn't matter what the inclement Cornish weather offered; their secret cove was beautiful with each month offering a different natural wonder. The pretty flowers that sprung to life in springtime, the bright sun dazzling and dancing on the turquoise waters in the summer. Then the harshness of the autumnal and winter months, they too held a certain beauty of the rugged coast. And the seals themselves! He smiled to himself thinking back to how excited he and Jodie were, even now as adults, when the first seal pups arrived each year, the circle of life. Feeling immensely privileged that this special place was his home, and regardless to what the future held, and where he and Jodie might end up, one thing he knew for sure was that he couldn't wait to stand right where he was, with Jodie and his baby, sharing the spectacular Seal Cove view with them both, as a family.

Feeling content that he was sharing this moment with his new horse, and now faithful friend, Xander, he squeezed his legs to indicate that their quiet moment was over.

"Come along now boy, it's time to check the sheep."

Trotting up the track towards the moors, Xander's ears pricked with anticipation of the gallop that was soon to come, and Theo thought that it wouldn't be long now before he and Jodie could ride their horses together. As the track levelled out and he was met with the open span of barren moorland, and with his mind settled, for the first time since he arrived home, he squeezed his legs to signal Xander could run. Fast and fearless, Theo and Xander thundered across the open ground. There were sheep to find.

Kate

Kate's boots crunched loudly on the gravel as she tentatively walked away from the security blanket of her trusty Land Rover and made her way over to Mrs Conrad's front door. She'd been apprehensive about coming, knowing full well that her past behaviour towards Jonah had been nothing other than ghastly. Every time she thought about it, she felt colour flush her cheeks with mortification and shame. And now he'd gone and saved her life. She could no longer hide away and pretend the last eight months had never happened. It was time to face him. It was time to both apologise and express her tremendous gratitude for his selfless bravery. Hesitantly lifting her hand to knock on the front door, she felt nausea rising within her. *Five minutes. You only need to be brave for five minutes. Say sorry, say thank you, say goodbye.* And with that mantra going round in her head, she tapped her knuckles on the wooden door.

"Kate, love, come on in," cried Mrs Conrad, welcoming her warmly and inviting her into her home. "He's in the kitchen, I'll take you through."

Kate liked the Conrads. She didn't know them well, but being almost neighbouring farmers, she'd seen them often out and about at the local feed store and livestock auctions and they always wished her and Jodie well. They had a good name within the farming community for helping any local farmer in need, as well as keeping top quality pigs. And she couldn't deny the genuine affection they held for Jonah when she saw them both at the hospital with him. She had seen it with her own eyes. Mrs Conrad never left his side, and she'd also been kind to Kate when she'd tried to visit him in hospital. Kate wondered if she would have been quite so friendly towards her if she knew just how badly she'd treated Jonah in the past.

Kate's heart thudded in her chest as soon as she saw him sitting at the kitchen table, and the usual flush of instant attraction filtered through her as she took in his black tousled hair, his gentle eyes and broad, muscular frame.

"Hello, Kate," he said, and she noticed his warm tone of voice, albeit a little bit guarded.

"Hi Jonah," she replied, trying to keep her own voice level and friendly.

Sensing the awkwardness between them, Mrs Conrad announced that the pigs wouldn't feed themselves! But with this, Jonah immediately rose from his chair.

"I'll feed the pigs, you've been busy all morning. Sit down and make yourself a cup of tea."

"You're supposed to be resting! And you're not to get those bandages dirty, you don't want that burn to get infected," she replied, and Kate detected the obvious motherly concern radiating out of her.

"I'll help," she chipped in, keen for something to do with herself. Anything would be better than standing awkwardly in the kitchen. "Jonah can tell me what to do. I'll do all the work," she assured her.

She watched Mrs Conrad cast her eyes over herself, and then Jonah. Acknowledging Jonah's subtle nod, she relented.

Kate silently followed Jonah to the piggery, and on his instructions, set about preparing the feed buckets for Mrs Conrad's batch of pigs to fatten, pigs for the show ring, and her two breeding sows. One was heavily pregnant, and one had a litter of nine five-week-old piglets. Each batch had different feeds, and amounts, in keeping with their needs, and Kate was rather impressed with how Mrs Conrad ran her little pig operation, and equally impressed that Jonah seemed to know the routine in meticulous detail. She worked quietly and efficiently, the only words spoken between them being Jonah's instructions. And then she got to Primrose, Mrs Conrad's prize-winning breeding sow, and her litter of piglets. She couldn't help herself, the gorgeous snuffling, grunting, playful piglets caused her to gasp out in delight.

"Oh, how adorable!" she squeaked, opening the latch to let herself into the pen to pour Primrose's feed into the trough. The piglets raced over to her, all jarring for her attention and fuss, all the while Primrose gobbled up her food, seemingly grateful that her boisterous babies were distracted, and she could eat her own food in peace.

"Primrose is super friendly," announced Jonah. "You can sit on the straw and play with them if you like!"

"Really?" replied Kate, instantly settling herself on Primrose's deep bed of golden straw, allowing the nosy piglets to clamber all over her.

Kate was so engrossed with the piglets and their silly little antics that she momentarily forgot why she was there. It wasn't until she looked up to see Jonah watching her, that her shame and self-imposed disgrace came flooding back.

Nestled amongst the piglets she knew the time had come. "I'm so very sorry, Jonah, for everything," she started.

"It's ok, Kate," he interrupted.

But before he could say anymore, Kate knew that it wasn't ok. What she'd done to him wasn't ok at all, and she would not let herself off the hook that easily.

"No, Jonah, no it's not," she said, looking right at him. She held his soft gaze for as long as she could, then embarrassment swept over her again, and she turned her attention back to the piglets before continuing.

"I was truly horrid to you. You know I was. You were nothing but kind and helpful to both me and Jodie and in return, I treated you terribly. I'm so sorry, Jonah. You did nothing wrong; it was all me. And I know it's not an excuse," she said, tentatively raising her eyes to meet his again briefly, "but with losing dad, the pressure of running the farm on my own, and then Jodie's pregnancy. Well, I took all of my frustrations out on you. And you didn't deserve that."

Jonah said nothing. What could he say? *Everything I've said is true,* she thought miserably.

"And I don't have the words to express how grateful I am for what you did for me in the fire. You saved my life Jonah," she ploughed on.

Jonah remained quiet, and in the awkward stillness of the piggery, she felt she had no more to say. She'd said her piece, and now it was time to leave. She carefully extracted herself from the pile of piglets and slipped out of Primrose's pen.

"If you ever need anything, Jonah, anything at all, you know where to find me," and then she turned on her heel to leave. She couldn't let Jonah see the tears welling in her eyes and her thudding, aching heart in her chest. She clambered into her Land Rover, carefully drove out of the farmyard, and then let go. Deep, heavy, ugly sobs poured out of her, and Flo, who'd remained snoozing in the car, gently placed her paw on her mistress's leg in comfort for the duration of the journey home.

Arriving home, Kate went straight into the kitchen to be met with Jodie singing away to the radio, baking up a feast. On hearing her arrival, Jodie turned to welcome her, and as Kate watched her expression change, she saw her sister almost physically feel her own heartbreak.

"Oh, Kate," she cried, dripping cake batter over the kitchen floor as she marched straight over to her and enveloped her in her arms.

Clinging on to her little sister, Kate's overwhelming emotions continued to flow. She heaved heavy sobs into her sister's golden ringlets and her shoulders ached with the emotional burden she'd been carrying for so long.

"I've been such a bitch," she hiccupped, between the swells of tears. "I think I love him, Jodie. How could I have been so horrid."

All the while Jodie smoothed her back and held her in her arms.

"He didn't say anything, not that I blame him," she continued, "I don't think I'll ever see him again," she stammered, causing more tears to stream relentlessly down her burning cheeks.

Kate didn't know how long Jodie held her in the kitchen, but eventually, her tears ceased and Jodie settled her down on a kitchen chair before preparing a cup of tea for them both.

Jodie clasped her hand between her own to comfort her.

"Everything is going to be ok, Kate," she tried to reassure her.

But Kate didn't think it would be. She'd disregarded and snubbed the one person who'd supported her during her time of need. She'd systematically ruined a potentially wonderful relationship, and she had no one to blame but herself.

Kate made her excuses to Jodie; she needed to shower and freshen up before heading out to check the cattle and mend a broken fence in the top paddock. Farmers were not given much time to wallow in self-imposed pity.

Standing under the hot water blasting out of her shower, Kate watched the soapy water filter down the drain, a symbol, she thought, of moving on. And she was at least grateful to have said her peace and she hoped, in one way or another, cleared the air between them and given them both some closure. I can do no more, she told herself firmly. I can't turn back the clock, I've admitted and apologised for my behaviour, now, I have to move on.

She stepped out of the shower feeling determined and confident. She would get dressed and get to work. Losing herself in her work, and her horses, with Flo at her side, is how she would get through this bleak patch in her life. Wiping the condensation off her bathroom mirror, she looked directly into her own eyes and said out loud, "You will get through this."

Just as she was slipping her warm fleece on over her head, she heard Jodie clambering up the stairs before bursting into her bedroom.

"Kate, Kate, Kate," she squealed. "He's here!"

Confused by her sisters excited manner, she stared at her with quizzical eyes.

"What are you talking about? Who's here?"

"Jonah! He's riding Jonty up the drive right now!" she squealed again.

Kate all but shoved Jodie out of the way to race into Jodie's bedroom where she could get a clear view of the farm's driveway.

"Oh my God, what the hell is he doing here?" she called out to Jodie, her voice laced with panic.

"You wait here," said Jodie, taking charge. "I'll go and find out. He might not be here to see you at all. I'm sure everything will be fine," she said, giving her a comforting pat on her arm before going downstairs to investigate.

Within minutes Jodie was huffing and puffing her way back up the stairs. "He's here to see you," she announced. "What do you want me to tell him? I'll ask him to leave if you don't want to see him. Just tell me what to say and I'll say it," said Jodie. And in that moment Kate realised how very lucky she was to have a sister like Jodie. No questions asked, she just had her back. And that fact alone filled her with confidence.

"I'll go and see him myself," she told her sister, then she quickly pulled her sister into her arms, and whispered, "Thank you, you're the best."

She mentally prepared herself for what might be to come as she slowly made her way down the stairs. Gripping the handle of her front door tightly, she took a deep breath, then swung her door wide open. And there he was, standing next to his handsome horse in the middle of her yard.

As soon as he saw her, he broke out a tentative smile, "Hello again, Kate. I thought that maybe," he said, pausing briefly, seemingly trying to find his words. "Maybe you and Artie might like to come riding with us?" he finished, then busied himself stroking his horse whilst he waited for her reply.

Curiosity swept through her as to what the offered ride might mean, and there was only one way she would find out for sure...

"I'll go and tack him up now."

Jodie

Jodie was busy setting the table for lunch when the oven timer beeped loudly, alerting her that the homemade Cornish pasties were ready. Reaching forward, she opened the kitchen window and delighted in seeing the year's first flecks of snow fluttering in the sky.

"Guys, lunch is ready," she called out across the yard, before swiftly closing the window tightly to keep out the freezing air.

By the time Kate, Jonah and Theo trudged across the yard and kicked their boots off in the hall, she'd placed the piping hot pasties on the table and whipped up steaming mugs of hot chocolate for them all.

"Mmmm, something smells delicious," said Theo, striding across the kitchen to give her a quick kiss before settling himself at the table.

Jodie felt herself glow on the inside when receiving his tender gesture. Sometimes she still couldn't quite believe that Theo was hers, and that his affectionate displays and intimate glances were just for her.

Once the hungry workers were tucking into their much-needed feast, Kate turned to her, and between mouthfuls, said, "Anything to report yet?"

With all eyes now on her, Jodie replied, "Argh, no!" The frustration was clearly audible in her voice.

It was the twenty first of December, one day past her due date, and no sign of the baby arriving anytime soon. She hadn't even had so much as a twinge. Theo had taken her for her midwife appointment last week and all was as it should be. All they could do now was wait until baby was ready. But she was so fed up with waiting! Nine months seemed like a lifetime to her, and to have passed her due date and still be without her baby was infuriating.

"How's the barn coming along?" she asked, eager for the distraction. Anything was better to literally counting down the minutes until the first sign, no matter how small, that the baby was on its way.

Kate launched into describing the progress they'd made over the past three weeks. All the debris and rubble had been cleared away, and the new concrete that had been laid two days ago was now set and the timber frames had been delivered this morning. The makeshift shelter was now securely erected in the paddock to ensure the horses had some protection from the harsh winter weather, and everything was coming along nicely. And all the while her sister talked enthusiastically about the rebuild, she watched Jonah, watching Kate. Jodie felt a warm fuzzy feeling bubbling away inside her as slowly, day by day, Kate and Jonah's friendship rekindled.

The fire had been one of the worst tragedies the farm had ever suffered, she knew that without a doubt. But deep down, she couldn't help but be a little bit grateful for it. She still felt terribly guilty for leaving Kate that day, and the fear of what might have happened if Jonah hadn't turned up when he did to save Kate still haunted her. But, although she would only ever admit this to herself, she could see that Kate was different now. Different in a good way. She was pleased to see her attitude towards Jonah had done a complete u turn, and she was finally treating him how he deserved to be treated. And Jonah, well, she thought, with a smile twitching on her lips, he's obviously forgiven her being such a horrible old bag because not only is he here every spare minute he has to help rebuild the barn, but he also can't keep his eyes off her!

Oooooh, what was that? She felt a dull ache sweep across her belly, then it was gone. She shifted on her seat, mulling over whether it was the baby, or just belly ache from her rich, all butter pastry pasty. She shifted her focus back to Jonah who was animatedly talking about something to do with one of Mrs Conrad's piglets. She'd clearly missed the joke along the way because everyone suddenly burst out laughing.

There it is again...

"Jodie, are you ok?" asked Kate, and suddenly she had three pairs of concerned eyes on her.

"I don't know," she admitted, suddenly embarrassed that she wasn't actually sure, and it might be a false alarm.

Seeing her unease, Jodie was grateful that Kate took charge of the situation. "Boys, I think I'd better stay with Jodie. Would you mind feeding the cattle and horses for me please? Better to be safe than sorry!"

Theo and Jonah jumped up, keen to be of help to the sisters, and the hopefully imminent arrival of the baby.

"I'll let you know if anything happens," Kate assured them both as they hastily pulled on their boots.

Jodie was grateful to stay inside her warm, cosy kitchen, as she watched the men hurry off to work amongst the heavily falling snowflakes out of the window.

And there it was again, a wave of pain swept across her stomach, and it was stronger than the last one. She put the kettle on whilst Kate busied herself tidying the kitchen table. Placing the tea pot on the table, another ache flooded through her, and this time she couldn't keep herself from running her hand across her belly to smooth the pain.

"Was that a contraction?" her sister asked eagerly.

"I think it was," she said tentatively, suddenly afraid of what was to come.

"Sit down, sit down," said Kate, immediately fussing over her like a mother hen. "We have to time them, that's what the midwife said."

Jodie did as she was told, and with her sister hovering, intermittently staring at her watch, then at her, she waited. And she didn't have to wait long before the next contraction arrived.

"Blimey," said Kate, that was quick. "I'm calling Theo."

Theo was at her side within ten minutes, and from that moment, she felt like she was in a whirlwind. It was decided that Jonah would stay at the farm to finish feeding the animals. He would meet them all at the hospital later. She was then bundled into the back of the car with her prepacked hospital case. Kate continuously asked what she could do to help, and Theo focused on driving them safely to the hospital in the ever-thickening snow. And all the while her fear was mounting as her contractions were coming on faster, and more painful than the last.

Being settled in a hospital bed, and the comforting reassurance from an experienced midwife telling her that she was in safe hands and that baby was definitely on its way, brought a sense of relief flooding through her. She was here, she was in expert hands, and finally, her baby was coming.

The midwife explained to her that she could only choose one person to stay with her during the delivery. She desperately wanted to pick Kate. She'd been her security blanket for so long. But she knew she couldn't. It wouldn't have been fair on Theo, and it was time for her to trust in Theo, just like she did her sister. Reluctantly, she watched her sister leave the room and clasped Theo's hand in her own, squeezing it tightly as the next wave of pain washed over her.

She was, hot, sweaty, and by god was she tired.

"Not long now, Jodie," reassured the midwife. All the while, Jodie was thinking that she had no more energy to give.

She felt Theo's hand carefully tuck her golden ringlets behind her ear, then slipped his hand in her own and give it a squeeze.

'Nearly there, I can see baby's head, push with the next contraction, baby's almost here," said the midwife.

Jodie gritted her teeth, bore down, and pushed with her every last ounce of energy she could summon. And then she heard it. The sound of her baby crying coupled with the midwife exclaiming her healthy baby had arrived.

"You have a son, Jodie!" announced the midwife.

She flopped back against her pillow, exhausted, and after watching the midwife clean and wrap her baby up in a soft, white blanket, she turned to Theo and saw that he had tears in his eyes. He lent forward and gently kissed her forehead.

"You did it!" he whispered. "We have a son!"

Her heart melted inside her with the thought that she and Theo, and their baby boy, were now a family.

"Who would like to hold him first?" offered the smiling midwife.

Jodie knew Theo was desperate to hold him, but when he indicated that she was to hold him first, she didn't refuse. Her moment was finally here and as selfish as it might seem, she wanted to be the first person to hold her own baby.

She shuffled her aching body into the most comfortable position she could manage as the midwife brought her baby over to her, and then he was in her arms. She held him as tightly as she dared, inhaled his intoxicating baby smell, and drank in every little detail of his cherubic face, his chubby little arms, and teeny tiny fingers.

After the midwife discreetly left them alone to enjoy their special moment together, she felt Theo rest his arm around her shoulders, and with his other hand, he gently stroked his son's cheek.

"Your turn now," said Jodie, holding the baby out to him.

As she watched the father of her son cradle him in his arms, her heart melted within her chest. Never, not even in her dreams, had she ever imagined the feelings that were swelling up inside her in that very moment. She wished that she could bottle them up and hold on to them forever, for right then, she had everything she'd ever wanted. Cocooned in the hospital delivery room was her perfect little family. She could hardly believe that she was now a mum!

A knock at the door broke the spell and brought her back down to reality.

"Are you ready for some visitors?" asked the midwife. "I have a very excited aunty out here!"

And Jodie was; she couldn't wait to show her baby off. "Yes! Send her in."

Kate bounced through the door, beaming from ear to ear, softly saying, "Congratulations," as she came straight over to her and wrapped her up in her arms, before whispering, "I'm so proud of you," in her ear.

Jodie sat back and watched Theo proudly hand over his son to Kate and she saw her face flush with love holding her baby nephew for the first time, "Oh Jodie, he's just perfect."

And then she saw Jonah tentatively peeking around the hospital door and she gestured eagerly for him to come in. And just like she'd done earlier in the day, she watched Jonah, watching Kate cradle her baby. The way he looked at Kate, was just the way Theo looked at her, and that fuzzy feeling came whooshing through her again.

"Have you thought of a name for him?" asked Kate, not looking away from the baby.

Jodie looked at Theo. They'd been discussing names for weeks, and they'd narrowed it down to two. And now, having met him, she knew exactly which name would be his. She only hoped that Theo would be in agreement with her.

"Timmy, we're going to call him Timmy," she announced, and she was grateful to see Theo's eyes light up whilst he nodded in agreement.

"Timmy," echoed Kate. "You're naming him after dad." And Jonah, sensing Kate's overwhelming emotions bubbling up inside her, placed his arm around her shoulders and tentatively pulled her towards him. Jodie watched Kate rest her head on his shoulder, still not taking her eyes off Timmy. Finally, thought Jodie, she has someone to lean on.

Suddenly concerned that her choice in name might be more tactless than meaningful to Kate, she asked, "Is that ok with you?"

For the first time since her sister held the baby in her arms, she looked up. Jodie could see tears welling in her sister's eyes as she stared right back at her.

"Of course," she gushed, "these are happy tears! Dad would be so proud of you, Jodie, and absolutely made up that you've chosen to name your son after him."

Jonah

It was Christmas Eve morning, the ground was thickly covered in snow, and Jonah and Jonty were down in the hills after checking the sheep. Like always, Jonah stopped to soak up the natural colours and beauty that surrounded him every day on Mr and Mrs Conrad's farm, tucked away in the little Cornish valley. Today offered him a gloomy sky, showing off every shade of grey imaginable, and the threat of more snow was not far away. The dim sky cast shadows from the trees lining the Conrads' boundaries and a comforting silence surrounded him during the early hour. He inhaled the fresh, chilly air deeply, relishing the ever-changing seasonal weather, and appreciating all it had to offer him.

"We'd better get going," he said out loud to his horse, "Mrs Conrad will have my breakfast ready soon!"

And he was right. As soon as he and Jonty set foot on the yard, the kitchen window flung open, and he was greeted by Mrs Conrad announcing his bacon butty was ready and waiting for him.

Chomping down on his doorstop wedge of freshly baked bread, and home reared bacon sandwich, Jonah notice Mrs Conrad subconsciously shifting from foot to foot rather nervously as she pottered about her kitchen making the tea.

Concerned, he asked her, "is everything ok?"

"I was just wondering," she stammered, "if you would be home this evening? I know you're off to see Kate soon..." she trailed off.

Mr Conrad had already given him a very subtle heads up that Mrs Conrad was hoping to do a family dinner for the three of them on Christmas Eve as they were invited to Kate's for lunch on Christmas day. Jonah couldn't quite believe his own luck that for the first time ever, he'd be spending time with people that he could now call his family at Christmastime. And there was no way that he would let Mrs

Conrad down, nor let her miss out on preparing her special Christmas Eve dinner, for him, the newest member of her family.

He quickly eased her worry. "Of course I'll be home!" he enthused, "I've borrowed Kate's trailer so I can box Jonty up instead of riding over to her. I'll be back in plenty of time, I promise." And he watched the concern ebb away from Mrs Conrad's face on hearing his confirmation that he would be there, and that she was without doubt his priority that evening.

They chatted contentedly together whilst finishing breakfast, and when he got up to take his leave, on the spur of the moment, he reached out and placed his arms around her affectionately, just like he would if she were his mum.

Driving over to Kate's, with Jonty safe and secure in the trailer behind, Jonah thought back to Kate's initial visit to the farm, all those weeks ago, and how far they'd come since then. He'd been able to forgive her cold, defensive behaviour with ease. He knew what it was like to be angry all the time. He knew what it was like to suffer unsurmountable grief, and quite frankly, her aloof, abrasive attitude had been nothing compared to his years as a teenager, when he had well and truly gone off the rails, and the later days of his early twenties when in all honesty he had taken part in some rather illegal dalliances. He'd come to the conclusion that although she'd hurt him at the time, with everything that she'd been going through, it was all understandable. And he decided that it was not in his best interest to cut off his nose to spite his face, when he did want to be friends with her again. More than friends if he was completely truthful with himself, but he'd settle for whatever she decided his being in her life was to be.

Kate was waiting for him when he arrived with Artie tacked up and ready. His black winter coat gleamed from Kate's meticulous grooming, and he stood tall and proud next to his mistress, just like he always did.

Kate chatted away as he unloaded Jonty from the trailer and prepared him for their ride, and Jonah appreciated how their friendship was blossoming. Since the fire, and the birth of baby Timmy, Kate's whole demeanour had changed. She was happy. And he presumed that this is what she must have been like before her whole world came tumbling down around her when she lost her father. He also privately hoped that his constant, unobtrusive presence over the last few weeks helping her rebuild her barn, not to mention his now permanent residence only ten miles away, offered her a sense of his commitment to her and dedication to forging their friendship.

"To the beach?" she asked.

"Definitely," he replied, excitement building in him with the thought of galloping hard and fast right alongside her.

As the horses veered off the sand dune track and onto the beach, the threatening snow finally began to fall. The biting wind whipped around them, the swelling waves crashed along the shoreline, and the snowflakes blurred the empty, barren beach. Jonah followed suit when Kate pushed Artie into a fast canter, and then before he knew it, the pair of them were galloping hell for leather across the snowy sand, with Kate's bright red hair bringing the only colour against the bleak backdrop of natural elements.

They stopped briefly at the top of Seal Cove point, but with the wintery weather obscuring any potential seal spotting that day, they headed for home. All too soon for Jonah, their Christmas Eve ride came to an end, and in what felt like no time at all, they were untacking their horses and grooming them down. With the plan being that Kate and Jonah would go riding on Christmas Day together, Jonty was to have a sleep over with Artie and Jonah was keen to help Kate settle him in, then prepare the feeds for all the horses in her temporary, makeshift tack room.

"Hey guys," called out Jodie, "I thought you might like these." She was carrying two steaming mugs of hot chocolate, complete with whipped cream and sprinkles on top. Handing them over, she scuttled back off to Timmy, and her warm kitchen; she had a Christmas feast to prepare!

Standing side by side, they sipped their drinks in silence, and in that moment,

Jonah physically ached with wanting to hold her in his arms. Determined not to push or do anything that might ruin their newly established friendship, but unable to shake the unyielding need to hold her, he gently shifted his weight. Those two inches now meant his arm gently rested up against hers, and she didn't move away. Instead, she slowly lent towards him and rested her head against his shoulder, just like she'd done in the woods. And he knew, right then, that she was fumbling through this unchartered territory, just like he was. That she was just as unsure of his feelings, as he was of hers. A calmness spread over him now, knowing that at some point, hopefully soon, he'd be holding her in his arms again. And with that knowledge, he told her that it was time for him to leave. Mrs Conrad was expecting him. They would see each other again tomorrow.

It was dark by the time he arrived home, and after being reassured by Mr Conrad that morning that he would do the evening check and feed of the animals, Jonah headed straight into the house. As soon as he stepped through the door, he was met with wafts of deliciousness of whatever Mrs Conrad was busy creating for their Christmas Eve dinner. On entering the kitchen, he felt liked he'd stepped into a private Christmas wonderland that Mrs Conrad had created just for them. Sprigs of holly, with bright red berries were hung from the ceiling, sparkly red and gold tinsel was strewn across the kitchen cupboards and twinkle lights adorned the kitchen window. The table was set with bright red crockery, crackers were sitting on their plates, a bottle of fizz was chilling in an ice bucket, and the flickering candles, dotted all over the kitchen, encased the Conrad's kitchen in a cosy, warm glow.

Mrs Conrad beamed up at him as soon as she saw him, and to Jonah, she embodied everything he'd ever pictured, and dreamed of, from a mother at Christmas. Her cheeks were rosy from the heat of her kitchen, and her eyes twinkled in delight as soon as she saw him. She wore a pretty green dress underneath her festive Christmas apron, and when she reached up to give him a welcoming kiss on his cheek, he inhaled her soft scented lavender perfume. She smelt like home.

"Welcome home, love," she said, gesturing for him to sit down and make himself comfortable.

Jonah and the Conrads chatted and laughed together all the way through their roast beef, with every trimming imaginable accompanying it. And it was not lost on Jonah, that for dessert, she'd created the most delicious chocolate pudding. The sponge was perfectly light, and the gooey chocolate sauce oozed out when she dished it up for them all, with a healthy dose of Cornish clotted cream on the side. His absolute favourite, and he was touched that she'd remembered.

Feeling fat, full and content, Jonah got up to help Mrs Conrad tidy up and do the dishes, and that in itself was immensely satisfying. He wanted it all. Every aspect of family life he wanted to share and take part in. Standing side by side at the kitchen sink, his hands dripping in greasy dishwater, he felt a wave of gratitude engulf him with finding the Conrad's.

Coffee and mints were to be taken in the sitting room, which just like the kitchen, was adorned in Christmas decorations, the log fire was roaring, and the six-foot Christmas tree took centre stage.

"Jonah, love," said Mrs Conrad. "We thought that you might like to put the star on the tree?" she asked, offering him the bright red, sparkly ornament.

Jonah was momentarily lost for words, and he felt his throat thicken with emotion at being included in such a special family occasion. Taking the star silently, he reached up and placed it carefully on the top of the Conrads' beautifully decorated tree.

"Perfect," praised Mrs Conrad. "Now you two sit down," she told the men. "I'll be back in two ticks," before disappearing up the stairs.

Relaxing in a comfy armchair, chatting to Mr Conrad, sipping his coffee, and warming his feet in front of the fire, Jonah thought that never before had he felt so utterly content. When Mrs Conrad returned, she was carrying a cardboard box.

"With us all being at Kate's tomorrow, Mr Conrad and I thought we'd give you your present this evening."

Jonah was stunned that after everything the Conrads had done for him, they'd even gone to the effort of getting him a present. He'd enjoyed Christmas shopping. It was a pleasure to actually have someone to buy presents for. And he hoped that Mr Conrad would appreciate the new shepherd's crook he chose for him, and that Mrs Conrad would like the beautiful woolly scarf, with matching gloves he'd got for her to keep her warm in the bitter winter weather.

He went to get up. "Yours are in my room, I'll just go and get them."

He noticed Mrs Conrad's cheeks go pink on hearing that he'd got her a Christmas present, but she gestured for him to stay sitting down.

"You stay there, love. I'm too excited for you to open yours first! I'm sorry it's not wrapped," she said, handing over the plain, cardboard box.

The box was heavier than it looked, and before he had chance to open it up himself, a little black nose poked out. The box wriggled on his lap, and before he knew it, the most adorable black and white collie pup clambered into his arms.

"Oh Mrs Conrad, she's beautiful," gushed Jonah, scooping the puppy up, kissing her soft, fluffy fur, and inhaling her delicious puppy scent.

"We thought that you might need your own working dog now that you're here to stay," offered Mr Conrad, watching him cuddle the pup.

Jonah's heart swelled inside his chest with the thoughtfulness and kindness that the two people, smiling broadly in front of him, had given him.

"She's just perfect, thank you," he replied.

"What will you call her?" asked Mrs Conrad.

Jonah soaked up the Christmas atmosphere encased within the little family farmhouse, and he mentally stored the image in his mind. He wanted to remember this moment forever.

"Eve," he announced. "Because you gave her to me on Christmas Eve, and she is without doubt, the best present anyone has ever given me."

He noticed Mrs Conrad's eyes were brimming with emotion, just like his own, and reaching out, he clasped her hand in his. "Thank you for everything."

Theo

Theo was in his mother's kitchen helping her prepare the chocolate yule log that she would be taking to Kate and Jodie's Christmas lunch the following day. Although Jodie was adamant that she could prepare and cook everything for their special Christmas feast herself, no one would hear of it. Both Mrs Stevens and Mrs Conrad would be bringing puddings, Theo had helped Jodie prepare all of the vegetables that morning, so all she needed to do tomorrow was cook, and he would be at her side to help her. Kate laid out the family Christmas crockery in the dining room but had relented after seeing Jodie's stricken face at her 'artistic attempts' and allowed Jodie to arrange the table, complete with crackers, candles, and sprigs of holly, just the way she liked it. And Theo had to agree. No one created a homely, festive atmosphere quite like Jodie did.

Ever since Timmy had arrived, Theo had been staying in Jodie's spare room to help her in any way that he could. They'd settled into a routine already. Jodie was up in the night with Timmy, but first thing in the morning, Theo would bring the contented, wide awake baby into Jodie. Whilst she fed him, he would go downstairs to make breakfast, then take it for Jodie to enjoy in bed. Once Timmy finished his morning feed, he slept soundly for two hours, allowing Jodie some much needed sleep, and he would then go over to his farm for his morning's work.

Today, he'd returned after vegetable peeling and lunch with Jodie to help his mum, and at his father's request. Apparently, his parents had something they'd like to discuss with him, alone.

Bang on four o'clock, just like he always did, his father appeared for his afternoon cup of tea and slice of cake. His mother and father glanced at each other, signalling that his mother was very much in on whatever his father wanted to discuss. And it surprised him that she hadn't mentioned anything the whole afternoon he'd been with her.

"Why don't we all sit down," said his mother, bringing over a fresh pot of tea and a plate piled high with flapjacks.

Theo did as instructed, curiosity piquing within him at what this family meeting was all about. He watched his father get up, rummage around in one of the kitchen draws then fish out a large brown envelope. Briefly looking at Mrs Stevens, and acknowledging her nod, he handed it over.

"This is for you," he announced. "Sort of a Christmas present, if you want it," he continued, seemingly embarrassed with the gesture of whatever it was inside the envelope.

Slowly, Theo opened the seal and pulled out the papers inside. The first showed a photocopied outline, in black and white, of the farm. He'd seen the picture before, many times, but on this copy, there was a large X marked just on the boundary between their farm and Jodie's.

"The west, top paddock," said his father, explaining what he could see on the paper, and where the X was marked. And then to his surprise, his father continued, "It's for you."

"What?" he stuttered.

"We thought that now you have Timmy, you and Jodie might like a home of your own. Your mother has made all the appropriate planning applications for you to convert the fallen down cattle shed into a house." He turned to his wife, smiling. "She did it as soon as she found out that Jodie was pregnant!"

"I hope you don't mind, Theo," said his mum, concern written all over her face that she somehow might have overstepped the mark.

Touched by her thoughtfulness and kind gesture, he replied, "No Mum, not at all."

"We thought that this way, you and Jodie would be able to access both farms easily. She would be only a five minute walk down her farm track from Kate, and you a fifteen minute walk from us.

Overwhelmed by his parents' generosity, he simply replied, "It's perfect, thank you."

"Of course, you'll have to discuss it all with Jodie," stated his father, "and it will take at least twelve months to build. You know you can both live with us, or if the plan is for you to move to Jodie's farm, that's fine by us too. But we wanted you to have the option of having your own home. The paddock itself is yours. The paperwork you're holding states that you are now the owner, so you and Jodie can decide, at any time, what you would like to do."

Theo was lost for words, and so he stood up, walked over to his parents, wrapped one arm around each of them, and held them tightly.

His mother kissed his cheek, and whispered, "Merry Christmas, darling."

Driving home, Theo was nervous about discussing his parents' gift with Jodie. Although thrilled with the idea himself, the thought of separating Jodie from Kate wasn't far from his mind, and he had no idea if she would ever want to leave her own home. But one thing was for sure, no matter where Jodie wanted to live, as soon as she allowed him too, he would live with her and Timmy, permanently.

Baby Timmy was wide awake when he arrived, and a grateful Jodie handed him over to him straight away. Making cranberry sauce and shortcrust pastry with a baby in her arms was proving rather difficult! He sat at the table with Timmy cradled in his arms and watched his beloved Jodie in her element. Her cheeks were rosy, her golden ringlets bobbed about her shoulders as she pottered about her kitchen. Contentment and happiness radiated from her. He didn't ever want to let her go.

And then, "Jodie, will you marry me?" quite unexpectedly popped right out of his mouth.

She had her back to him, and he watched her stop what she was doing, her hands, covered in flour and butter, paused mid-air as she digested what he'd just said. And in that brief moment, he also digested what he'd just said, quickly concluding, that yes, he very much wanted her to be his wife, if she'd agree to it.

Slowly, she turned to face him, her bright blue eyes dancing, a beaming smile lighting up her pretty face, and she said, "Really? You want us to get married?"

"Yes," he said sincerely. "Yes, I do Jodie. I want you, me, and Timmy to be a family. So, what do you think?"

"Yes!" she squealed, before throwing her arms around him and planting a kiss on his lips.

He couldn't quite believe what had just happened. He only found out he was going to be a father just over three months ago, and now, here he was holding baby Timmy in his arms, and engaged to his beautiful Jodie. And then it hit him. *Oh my god, I haven't got her a ring!* He noticed a ball of string on the table that Jodie had been using for wrapping presents. He carefully placed Timmy into his carry cot, then he snipped off a piece of string. Taking her hand, he tied the string around her finger and carefully snipped the ends off with the scissors.

"I'm so sorry, Jodie, it was a little bit spur of the moment," he said, slightly abashed by his faux pas. "I promise we'll go ring shopping soon."

Jodie clasped his hands within her own. "This is perfect, Theo. I don't need any other engagement ring except for this one," she said, giggling, showing off her finger. "All I need is you."

He pulled her close to him and held her tightly, inhaling her familiar scent. *She said yes!*

Breaking away from him when Timmy began to get restless in his cot, she noticed the brown envelope on the table. "What's that?" she asked, gently rocking her baby to sooth him.

Buoyed with confidence that she was now to be his wife, Theo pulled out the paperwork and told her all about his parents' generous gift, and after listening carefully to everything he had to say, to both his surprise and delight, she said, "We get to build our very own house! Exactly how we want it to be?"

"That's pretty much the idea of it, yes," he replied, basking in her enthusiasm.

"Oh Theo, how exciting. I can design my own kitchen!"

"Yes, you can," he said, thinking how beautiful she would make their home. And just when he thought he was home and dry, he saw her face fall.

"But what about Kate?" she questioned, her eyes filled with worry. "I can't leave her. I've never been apart from her, and she'll be in this big old farmhouse all on her own with only Flo for company."

She paused briefly, seemingly lost in her own thoughts, before continuing, "And who will cook for her! She's a terrible cook! She'll live off toast and sandwiches if she's left to her own devices!" she said, with a look of horror on her face.

Theo tried to choose his words carefully because he knew that when it came to Kate, Jodie would always put her first. She'd been the mother figure she'd never had, and her constant support during the loss of her father, not to mention how she'd supported her wholeheartedly throughout Jodie's pregnancy. The sisters held a loyalty to each other that far surpassed most siblings, and he knew that he must never ask anything of Jodie that might cause her any anxiety with regards to Kate.

"It's going to be at least twelve months until we get married and our house will be ready to move into," he started, and noting that she was listening intently to what he had to say, he continued. "You and Timmy will still be living here up until that point, and even then, if you feel you're not yet ready to move, we can wait until you are. You will only ever be within a short walk away from each other, and maybe she could come up to our house for her meals?"

He watched her posture relax as she processed everything he said, which clearly had the desired effect when she suddenly blurted out, "We're getting married!"

Kate

Kate's shrill alarm bleeped loudly in the silence of her house. Already awake, she flicked it off immediately. Jodie would not be happy if she woke a sleeping Timmy! She slipped out of bed and drew back her curtains to see that yesterday's heavy snowfall had finally ceased. The dark sky was clear, and the moon illuminated her snow-covered farmyard.

It might be Christmas Day, but she still needed to feed the animals, so hastily dressing in her warm, fleece lined clothes, she skipped downstairs with Flo at her heels and headed into the crisp dawn air. She was on a tight timescale today. Even though she and Jodie had prepared everything they could yesterday, there was still lots to do before everyone arrived for their Christmas lunch, not to mention squeezing in a quick ride with Jonah before the festivities began.

The thought of Jonah sent tingles down her spine, and anticipation swirled within her at the thought of spending the whole day with him. She'd barely slept a wink last night. Round and round her mind went over every meticulous detail about their ride, and their moment in the tack room, which still brought butterflies to her stomach.

She loaded up her trusty Land Rover with cattle feed, then set off across her farm track. They were waiting eagerly for her at the gate, keen for their breakfast, just like they always were. After heaving the heavy bags of feed into their troughs, she climbed up onto the wall to survey her farmland. With Flo at her heels, and the only sound being that of the cattle munching their feed, she breathed in the frosty air, and said good morning to her dad.

"I wish you were here," she told him out loud. "Our first family Christmas with baby Timmy. I know you and Mum will be watching over us. Love you, Dad." Then she jumped off the wall, climbed into her truck and trundled back to the yard as the weak wintery sun began to trickly through the shadowy sky.

Her heart skipped a beat when she saw Jonah waiting on the yard when she returned. He was early.

As if reading her mind, as soon as she'd switched off the ignition to her Land Rover, he strode over and said, "I hope you don't mind me turning up early I finished our animals sooner than expected, and…well I wanted to show you my Christmas present from Mr and Mrs Conrad."

Kate noticed that he was trying, and failing, to keep the excitement out of his voice. And she was secretly thrilled that he'd chosen her to share in his excitement about whatever this Christmas present might be.

"I'm pleased you're here," she said, then saw his eyes fill with relief that he hadn't imposed on her. "So, what is it?"

He beckoned for her to follow him to the car. She waited expectantly as he opened the door and reached inside, and then proud as punch, he handed her the most adorable fluff ball of a collie puppy.

"Oh, Jonah! What a Christmas present. You lucky thing!" she gushed.

"Kate, meet Eve!"

"Hello, Eve," she whispered, as she nuzzled the little pup. "Just wait until Jodie gets her hands on you!" Then turning to Jonah, "Do you think I should leave Flo behind when we go riding so she can help Jodie look after her?"

"Mrs Conrad said I could take her home and she'd watch her for me, but if you think Jodie won't mind, then I'll leave Eve in her capable hands, and Flo's!"

"Of course, she won't mind! You'll be lucky to get her back once Jodie sets her eyes on her! Come on, let's go and introduce Eve to everyone," she said, leading the way to her home.

As predicted, Jodie, and Theo, who'd returned from feeding his own cattle, were more than happy to look after Eve. And Flo, seemingly very taken with the miniature version of herself, glued herself to Eve's side. After being plied with Jodie's whipped cream hot chocolates and bacon sandwiches and after Jodie had brought Jonah up to speed on the happy news of her engagement, Kate and Jonah left the warmth of her kitchen to tack up their horses. Kate noted that her usually loyal dog barely looked up when she left! *Puppies,!* she thought. *They turn us all to mush, even hard-working farm dogs!*

Without the distraction of Eve, Kate now struggled to keep her eyes off Jonah. She quietly went about her business of grooming and tacking up Artie, but every chance she got, she couldn't help herself but sneak a peak at the intriguing man beside her. And when they both reached for the dandy brush, and his hand knocked against hers, she felt like she'd been zapped by a lightning bolt. To hide her blushing cheeks, she'd bent down to pick out Artie's hooves, and to distract herself from her wandering mind, she announced to Jonah that she'd offered to check Theo's moorland sheep whilst out on their ride, and she hoped he didn't mind.

Jonah took the lead when the track narrowed, leading them towards the moors. This provided Kate with the perfect opportunity to stare openly at him, without him noticing! She liked how good he looked on a horse; it was like he blended seamlessly into his saddle, and he was just meant to be there. Then there was his natural gift with how he was around them and how he connected with them. Kate thought very highly of that. And then she thought, with a twinge of guilt, about his kind, caring and forgiving nature. He'd helped her in any which way he could after the fire, and she was grateful for it. She was beginning to realise how much easier her life was when she allowed people to help her. She didn't have to do it all on her own, and Jonah was very much someone who she was enjoying sharing the load with. And she hoped that the few times she'd popped over to the Conrads' farm to help either Mrs Conrad with the pigs, or Jonah with the stock, he'd recognise that what little spare time she had, she was willing to share it helping him. *A relationship is give and take,* she noted to herself.

The moorland was coated in a thick layer of snow, and Kate enjoyed the sound of the horses' hooves trudging through it as they plodded along counting the sheep. With the bitter wind picking up, and all sheep present and correct, she and Jonah, chatting in a companionable way, headed home. When they reached Seal Cove, she stopped Artie and soaked up the familiar view.

"It never gets boring, does it," said Jonah, openly appreciating the view just as much as she did.

Kate climbed out of Artie's saddle and tied him up to the post, then gestured for Jonah to follow suit.

"Let's get out of the wind for a moment and see if we can spot some seals!" she said, and Jonah followed her down the secret path.

"Look, down there," she said, pointing to the two seal heads she could see bobbing in the water below.

She watched his gaze follow her outstretched finger, and then his lips twitched into a smile.

"Of all the places I've visited across the world," said Jonah, "your little secret cave is the most beautiful place I've ever been."

When she turned to face him, she could see the sincerity in his eyes, and she held his gaze. Her heart thudded in her chest, and on that freezing cliff top, she felt a tingling spread within her when Jonah held his hand out to her. Slipping her hand into his, he gently pulled her closer to him, then the next moment she felt his warm lips brushing across her own. She didn't know how long he held her in his arms, whilst they sat in comfortable silence, watching the seals, but her legs were stiff, and her hands were numb when they finally parted and followed the path back up to their horses.

Arriving back on the yard, and after turning their horses out into the paddock, Jonah said, "I have something for you."

She waited whilst he went to his car, and she saw him retrieve a present wrapped in Christmas paper. Excitement as to what it might be bubbled up inside her when he handed it over to her.

"Merry Christmas, Kate."

And she was pleased to be able to take the small, wrapped gift she had for him out of her coat pocket.

"And Merry Christmas to you too," she replied, handing over his present.

He waited for her to open hers first. Her numb fingers opened the paper as carefully as they could, and then her breath caught in her throat on seeing his thoughtful, handmade gift.

"Oh Jonah, it's beautiful, thank you" she exclaimed, then reached up to kiss his freezing cold cheek to ensure he knew just how much she appreciated his wooden, hand-carved plaque of a horse and Artie's name.

"It's to go on his new stable when it's built," he said, shyly.

And then it was her turn to watch him open his present. She felt herself glow from head to toe with his immediate reaction of surprise and delight.

"It's perfect, thank you Kate," he replied, holding up the miniature brass plate with Jonty's name engraved on it to attach to his bridle. Then taking her hand, he continued, "Let's go inside, it's freezing!"

It wasn't long before the guests arrived, and soon they were all tucking into roast turkey with all the trimmings. Kate keenly voiced how wonderful it was and her appreciation for the hard work Jodie had put in behind the scenes to create such a feast, and all with a new-born baby!

As per Jodie's instructions, after dinner drinks, along with homemade chocolate truffles, would be taken in the sitting room, so their beautifully decorated tree could be appreciated by everyone. They could enjoy the warmth of the fire, and sing Christmas carols.

Once everyone was settled and comfy, Theo brought out his guitar and sang *O Holy night*. It had been a long time since Kate had heard Theo sing, and along with everyone else in the room, she listened intently as his beautiful voice filled her cosy sitting room. Theo then played *Rudolph the Red-Nosed Reindeer* and *Jingle bells* for everyone to sing along too, and just as they were deciding what he should play next, Mrs Conrad surprised her by asking Jonah to sing.

Kate noticed the colour rise in his cheeks at being put on the spot like that, but Mrs Conrad's smile seemed to make any hesitation on his part fade away, and he agreed to her request.

Kate felt herself sit more upright, alert to what was to come. *He can sing as well?*

Theo began strumming the chords to *In the Bleak Mid-winter*, and then there it was. Jonah's powerful, tenor voice pierced the silent room and sent tingles down her spine. *Blimey, he really can sing!* And she felt a rush of affection for him on finding out his hidden talent.

"You've got competition now, Theo!" called out Mr Stevens.

Theo beckoned Jonah to join him in front of the fire. "How about a duet!"

Together, the men sang *Deck The Halls*, and their voices blended so perfectly you'd think they'd sung together forever.

The happy little gathering cheered when the carol came to an end, and, blushing after his time in the spotlight, Jonah left Theo's side to make his way over to Kate.

"You have quite the voice," she praised, as he smiled bashfully.

Sitting beside her on the sofa, with his arm resting around her waist, she lent her head on his shoulder. She took in the joyous scene before her and smiled quietly to herself. Her whole family and closet friends were all cocooned in her festively decorated home. Flo and Eve were cuddled up in front of the fire together, and her guests were chatting and laughing amongst themselves. Mrs Stevens was cradling baby Timmy with Mr Stevens watching over them, as proud as any grandparents could be. Jodie and Theo were to be married! Mr and Mrs Conrad were eagerly cooing over the baby too, and Kate knew how very happy they were now they had Jonah in their life, completing their own little family. And not only did they have Jonah, but so did she. The lovely, kind, caring man, sitting right next to her, was hers. And she thought to herself, *what an exciting future we have ahead of us!*